George V. Higgins was a lawyer in the Massachusetts Attorney General's office, in the Organized Crime section and the Criminal Division, and an Assistant United States Attorney, in Boston. He then founded his own private practice, defending Watergate conspirator G. Gordon Liddy and Black Panther Eldridge Cleaver. Described as 'the Balzac of the Boston underworld', he wrote more than twenty novels, including a number of lowlife masterpieces constructed almost entirely out of pitch-perfect dialogue. He died in 1999.

By George V. Higgins

The Friends of Eddie Coyle
The Digger's Game
Cogan's Trade
A City on a Hill
The Friends of Richard Nixon
The Judgment of Deke Hunter
Dreamland
A Year or So with Edgar
Kennedy for the Defense
The Rat on Fire
The Patriot Game
A Choice of Enemies
Style vs. Substance
Penance for Jerry Kennedy
Imposters
Outlaws
The Sins of the Fathers
Wonderful Years, Wonderful Years
The Progress of the Seasons
Trust
On Writing
Victories
The Mandeville Talent
Defending Billy Ryan
Bomber's Law
Swan Boats at Four
Sandra Nichols Found Dead
A Change of Gravity
The Agent
At End of Day

COGAN'S TRADE

George V. Higgins

An Orion paperback

First published in Great Britain in 1974 by
Martin Secker & Warburg Limited.
This paperback edition published in 2012 by Orion Books
an imprint of The Orion Publishing Group Ltd
Orion House, 5 Upper Saint Martin's Lane
London WC2H 9EA

An Hachette UK company

3 5 7 9 10 8 6 4 2

A CIP catalogue record for this book is
available from the British Library.

ISBN: 978 1 4091 3753 5

Typeset by Input Data Services Ltd, Bridgwater, Somerset

Printed and bound by CPI Group (UK) Ltd, Croydon, CRO 4YY

The Orion Publishing Group's policy is to use papers
that are natural, renewable and recyclable products and
made from wood grown in sustainable forests. The logging
and manufacturing processes are expected to conform
to the environmental regulations of the country of origin.

www.orionbooks.co.uk

COGAN'S TRADE

1

Amato in a gray suit with a muted red stripe, textured pink shirt with his initials on the left French cuff, a maroon and gold tie, sat at the kidney-shaped, walnut veneer desk and stared. 'I got to give it to you,' he said, 'you're a great-looking couple of guys. Come in here about four hours late, you look like shit and you stink. The fuck, you look like you just got out of jail or something.'

'His fault,' the first one said. 'He was late. I stood around there and I waited for him.'

Both of them wore black boots with red suede inserts. The first one wore an army-green poncho, a frayed gray sweater and faded blue jeans. He had long hair, dirty-blond, and mutton-chop sideburns. The second one wore an army-green poncho, a gray sweatshirt and dirty white jeans. He had long black hair that reached his shoulders. He had the beginnings of a black beard.

'I hadda get my dogs in,' the second one said. 'I got fourteen dogs, there. Takes me a while. I can't, I can't just go off some place, leave them dogs out.'

'You're all covered with hair, too,' Amato said. 'You been backing them dogs up to you, I guess.'

'Comes from beating off, Squirrel,' the second one said. 'I come out, I haven't got your advantages, nice business waiting for me, all that good shit. I got to hustle.'

'"Johnny" around here,' Amato said, 'you can call me "Johnny" here. Most of the help calls me "Mister," but you can call me "Johnny." That'll be all right.'

'I'll work on that, Squirrel, I really will,' the second one said. 'You got to make allowances for me, you know? I, like I just got out of fuckin' jail. My head's all fucked up. I got to readjust to society, is what I got to do.'

'You couldn't've got somebody else,' Amato said to the first one. 'This item looks like shit and he don't have no manners. I got to put up with shit like this?'

'I could've,' the first one said, 'but you asked me, you know, get somebody that was all right. Russell, here, he's maybe kind of a wise ass, but he's all right if you can stand him.'

'Sure,' Russell said, 'and a guy like you, he wants something done, hasn't got the stones, do it himself, I think he oughta try pretty hard, too.'

'I really don't like this prick,' Amato said to the first one. 'He's too fuckin' fresh for my blood. How about going out and getting me a nice tough nigger? I don't think I can stand this cocksucker long enough to tell him what I want.'

'Russell, for Christ sake,' the first one said, 'willya shut the fuck up and stop jerking the guy's chain? He's tryin' to do us a favor.'

'I didn't know that,' Russell said. 'I thought he wanted us to do him a favor. That the straight shit, Squirrel? You tryin', do me a favor?'

'Get the fuck out of here,' Amato said.

'Hey,' Russell said, 'that's no fuckin' way, talk to a guy. The fuck you sell driving lessons to people, you go around talking to a guy like that?'

'This thing I got in mind,' Amato said, 'the two guys I get to do it're gonna cut up about thirty, I figure. Thirty K. Shitbirds like him, Frankie, shitbirds like him I can buy for eighty cents a dozen, they throw in another free. Get me somebody else, Frankie. I'm not gonna put up with this kinda shit.'

'Remember them habes we had?' Frankie said.

'Habes,' Amato said, 'what habes? We had about nine hundred habes. Every time I turn around that monkey's pulling out something else I got to sign. What habes?'

'They, the ones they bring us down for,' Frankie said. 'The federal ones.'

'On the line-up thing,' Amato said, 'yeah. The time that big coon come after me.'

'Long Tall Sally,' Frankie said.

'I dunno what his name was,' Amato said. 'We didn't have no nice conversation or anything. He was just trying to get my pants off and I was just trying to stop him from getting my pants off, is all. 'Jes hold still there a minute, white boy, I'm gonna shove all my good time right up your sugah ass.' Fuckin' guy. He had white lipstick on.'

'The next night he wasn't there,' Frankie said.

'The next night I wasn't there,' Amato said. 'If I had've been that fuckin' nigger wouldn't've, boy. I got Billy Dunn a wood chisel for that fucker, he was gonna grab him in the yard if I was there.

3

Fuckin' dumb screws, can't always depend on them guys showin' up when you need them like that, guy's liable to learn a new way, he's not careful.'

'You were in Norfolk,' Frankie said.

'I was in Norfolk,' Amato said. 'Sit there all day listening to some kid make a fuckin' asshole outa my goddamned lawyer, all I can think about's what Billy's gonna do to that coon, I get back there, and then it turns out, I'm going to Norfolk. Only thing I see that night, there's this nun in a gray thing, there, wants to know, do I wanna learn the fuckin' guitar.'

'I know her,' Russell said. 'She's all over the place. She was up to Concord once. I said to her, I said: 'Sister, I wanted to play the guitar, I would've grabbed a fuckin' guitar.' After that she left me alone. Lot of the guys liked her, though.'

'That night the nigger was in the hospital,' Frankie said.

'Good,' Amato said. 'I hope he fuckin' *died*.'

'Nope,' Frankie said, 'but I seen him. He was missing about three feet of skin off his fuckin' head.'

'Hey,' Amato said.

'Him,' Frankie said, nodding his head toward Russell.

'No shit,' Amato said.

'Peeled him like a fuckin' orange,' Frankie said.

'More like pulling bark off a fuckin' tree,' Russell said. 'Guy had skin like nothing I ever seen.'

'He came after you?' Amato said.

'Somebody sure did,' Russell said, 'somebody looked to me like he hadda be the biggest chungo bunny inna world, come after me. I had this blade there, another guy I meet onna way over, he told me, I give him a hundred out of my thing there and he had this blade for me. Said I was probably gonna need it. I bet I wasn't in

4

there ten minutes and that nigger's coming after me. Didn't do it again, though.'

'That's how come,' Frankie said. 'He's a prick but he's got all the moves.'

'He clean?' Amato said. 'Both you guys clean?'

'*Frankie,*' Russell said, 'you been *using* something?'

'Shut the fuck up, all right, Russell?' Frankie said. 'Yeah. I haven't had anything but booze since I get out. Not that much booze, either. Mostly beer. I been waiting for payday, I start in on the VO and other stuff.'

'You're on pills,' Amato said. 'You're in, you're on pills. I seen you, don't forget. You were beating the hell out of them yellowjackets.'

'John,' Frankie said, 'the yellowjackets were there. I didn't see nobody serving no beer. I took what there was. I haven't had none of that stuff since I was out.'

'How about him?' Amato said.

'*Gee*, Squirrel,' Russell said, '*I* wouldn't take nothing. I, ah, I probably had a couple quarts of Ripple and some grass, and I might've had one or two dime bags once or twice, but I just snort them, you know? It's not like I was using something. I go to Cub Scouts, you know? And they pat you down, there, they start teaching you how to tie them knots and everything.'

'Smack,' Amato said to Frankie. Frankie shrugged. 'I ask you to find a guy for me and I got this thing, and all I got to do is do it and we get some very nice money. All I got to do is find two guys that can do a fairly simple thing without fucking it up, and this is the best you can do for me. A fuckin' junkie. And I'm supposed to just let you guys go in there and you're gonna go in and once and for all you're gonna fuck it up, a job that's never gonna come around again in a million years. I don't want to have a whole lot of *fun* with this thing, you know, because I hadda go out and get a guy that looked all right when I got him and then he goes in and he's on the fuckin' nod or something. I want the goddamned money. That's what I need.'

'Squirrel,' Russell said, 'when I was a little kid I used to take off on Cheracol. I didn't have any trouble. When I was working for my Uncle, I used to have to go down in holes for him, you know? The carbon black on my face and go down in them holes with a forty-five in my hand and a knife in my fuckin' teeth and I went into them tunnels. Every day I went in them tunnels. If there wasn't anything in the tunnel, that was a good day. Not so good days, there's probably only a big fuckin' snake in there or something that wants to eat you. Kinda bad days, there's some skinny dink in there with a gun, tryin' to kill you. Bad days was when the dink did it, or there was a piece of wire in there and you didn't happen, you weren't paying attention or something and it's rigged up to something that blows up pretty quick, or else there's a punji stick in there with a whole lot of dink shit on it under your hand and you go into your basic blood poisoning extra quick.

'I didn't have no bad days,' Russell said. 'I was in them tunnels almost two years and I didn't have no bad days. I wasn't buying up Mustangs and teaching little dumb shits to drive, but I didn't have no bad days, either.

'The thing of it is, *Squirrel*,' Russell said, 'when I was having them days, I didn't know for sure at the time that I wasn't gonna have a bad one, you know? I started out, I thought it was all just a matter of balls. I don't wanna hurt your feelings or anything, but I always had the balls, you know? And I thought, I felt pretty good, because I thought that's all it was and I had them so I was all right. Then I see, I seen them cart out a couple guys that went in there and put them in the green bags, you know? And a couple of them, they didn't have no balls when they come out, on account they didn't have no luck, they went in that time, and no cocks either, and that carbon black, don't do a thing for cuts and stuff. Fuckin' booby traps go right through it, like it wasn't even there.

'So that gets me to thinking,' Russell said. 'I'm no good at thinking. But that gets me to thinking, and I see, well, I'm in the shit, is what I am, and I can't personally do nothing about it. All I can do is, I can have the balls and the luck, but the only thing I know about is the balls. I just can't have no bad days. Only, I don't know no way to do that. So, I used to come out, and I know, tomorrow I go in again, and the only thing I can think about is, I used up another day. That's all. So I smoke something. And it helped.

'Then I start looking at them other guys,' Russell said. 'I see them, I was still thinking, and they're all, most of them, at least're smoking. And them guys that're doing the grass, you know? Very heavy on it, and they slow down some. I was, I was keeping track of things. I could see it happening to me, it was happening to them, I got it a little bit and I begin to see, that's what, them other guys, they started on it, it was probably just a little bit for them, too, when they start. You start forgetting things. All you want, you don't care about things, you know? Very funny thing. And then, some of the guys that're older, they drink a lot. And pretty soon they're sick a lot. And that's bad. Their hands shake. They're not paying attention either. And you get in there, there's the wire or the dink or something, well, you're gonna have to have a lot of time to think about it or else you're not gonna have no time at all. You can't let yourself get slow.

'So I try the horse,' Russell said. 'You got to have something.

7

So I get some of that nice white shit, and what I did was, I used it after, right? *After* I come out again. I haven't got to go back in tonight. First I snort it. Then, a couple times I did it the other way, but mostly I snort it. But I used it. And I liked it.

'Okay,' Russell said, 'it don't, it makes you feel great, but it don't actually do nothing for you, you know that. When you're in there, doesn't protect you at all. But you been in, and you got out, and you got to go back in again and you don't want to think about that, maybe you're not gonna bring yourself out, you go in again, use up all your luck thinking. So then it's very fuckin' nice. Don't slow you down. Just makes you feel good, and that's what I was after.'

'Sure,' Amato said, 'and that's what you're gonna be after when you're getting ready to go in on this thing I got, and you're gonna get it and you're gonna be flying and you're gonna go in stoned up to your ass and some poor bastard's gonna start hollering or something and he's gonna get shot, and a very good thing that a kid in his fuckin' right mind couldn't fuck up is gonna get fucked up. That's exactly what I'm afraid of.'

'He'll be all right, John,' Frankie said.

'*Maybe* he'll be all right,' Amato said. 'Maybe he won't be all right. Maybe *you* won't be. I don't want nobody getting hurt on this. There's nothing, there's no reason why anybody oughta get hurt on this, the guys that go in or the guys that're in there when the guys go in. This's money, just money, nothing else. No fuckin' *shit* and stuff that's gonna get everybody all pissed off and everything. It was something that was gonna be around, it was something like that, all right, I could maybe take a chance. I could take a couple guys that I was afraid'd maybe cock off and wreck it, and take their word for it, they're gonna be all right. So all right, they go in, and they cock off and wreck it, it was a bank or some-thing, it's gonna be there next week for two guys that've got more sense, all right. But this isn't. It's not like that. You fuck it up, it's fuckin' gone, it's gonna disappear. I got to think about this. I got to be sure. I'm gonna talk to some people. I'm gonna take my time about this thing, as much time I got, anyway.'

'John,' Frankie said, 'I need dough. I was in the can a long time and I haven't found anything. You can't fuck around with me like this.'

'My friend,' Amato said, 'my wife, Connie? Makes great roast pork. She stuffs it, you know? It's really great. The other night she makes roast pork. First time since I been home. I couldn't eat it. I told her, I said: "Connie, don't make no pork for me, ever again." But I used to love it, I always said it's the best thing she makes, and she's a good cook. I mean, a really good cook. That's why she's so fuckin' fat all the time, she likes to eat and she likes to cook and she cooks great and she eats it. "Bacon," I said, "ham, I don't care if it does come off a pig. But no kind of pork. You make baked beans, all right? Don't gimme none with the pork on it. The beans I'll eat. Not the pork." And, well, I went down the clamstand and I ate in my fuckin' car, and I haven't, until a month ago I didn't eat with my family for almost seven years. I still ate down the clamstand. Something got fucked up once, you remember that? I picked a wrong guy for something, everybody's in a hurry, we got to move, we need the dough, this and that, he'll be all right, and I, it, I was worse'n the rest of you. So we take him, and I knew, he's a guy I'm really not sure about. I couldn't tell you what it was, I just knew it, this was a wrong guy. But I take him anyway. And he *was* a wrong guy, and I eat greasy, shitty pork, seems like every day, almost seven years, and my kids're growing up and my business, it's all right, it's not doing as good as it should be, and I'm in the can, and now, I can't get that back, you know? So now, I can't eat my favorite things any more, because they remind me, I'm, from now on I'm taking my time, and that's all there is to it. No, I don't care about you, what's bothering you. We can do something, great, we'll do something. If we can do it safe and without fucking up something that's really good and getting ourselves in the shit again. But I ate the last fuckin' pork I'm ever gonna eat. I had my last fuck-up. Call me Thursday. Thursday I'll know. I'll let you know.'

2

Russell stopped about four feet from Frankie on the second underground platform of the Park Street MBTA station. 'All right,' he said, 'I'm here. We going out there or what?'

Frankie leaned against one of the red and white pillars. 'Depends,' he said.

'Don't depend on me,' Russell said. 'I been up since quarter five. I'm *all* beat to shit. And I also, I got a chance to get laid if I don't go out there.'

'Don't people get laid at night any more?' Frankie said. 'My sister, we're kids, you couldn't keep Sandy inna house at night if she was tied up. Now she's out Tuesday and Wednesday afternoons. I been there five weeks, she's never home them days.'

'Must be a fireman,' Russell said, 'night guy inna fire station. Young guy, too, she's not going out, weekends.'

'Or a fuckin' cop,' Frankie said. 'It'd be the same thing with a cop. I said to her: "None of my business, Sandy, I just hope you're not rolling around with some fuckin' cop, is all." She looks at me. "Why?" she says. "What've you guys got that cops haven't?" I pity that kid.'

'You oughta pity yourself,' Russell said.

'I do,' Frankie said. 'She never had a clean shot, though. She always got around pretty good, I don't mean that. She just never hadda clean shot.'

'Nobody ever had a clean shot,' Russell said. 'What the fuck else is new? I was talking to this girl, she wants me to come over there this after. I said to her, look, I hadda be some place. What's the matter, tonight? She's gotta work. She gets off late. I don't care. I been up late myself before. She's a nurse. She says: "Look, I'm gonna wash old men's asses and everything all day. Then I'm gonna be out on my feet. You think I wanna get laid, after that? That what you think? I don't."'

'That oughta be something,' Frankie said. 'I can just see what kind of broad she's gonna be, you can screw off an ad inna paper. Beautiful. Probably got a couple handfuls of broken glass in there.'

'Look,' Russell said, 'you ought to know. I was pounding sand up my ass almost four years. I would've fucked a snake, I could've got somebody, hold it for me. These broads, okay, you wouldn't want to rape them if you saw them, you know? But they got the fuckin' plumbing.'

A badly coordinated heavyset man appeared on the southerly platform across the tracks. He wore white coveralls and carried a blue plastic pail. He turned his back and stared at the tile wall. He put the pail down. He put his hands on his hips. On the wall in red spray paint were irregular letters eighteen inches tall. They

12

read: SOUTHIE EATS IT. He stooped and removed a steel brush and a can of solvent from the pail.

'I wished I could look at things like that,' Frankie said. 'I can't seem to get my mind on anything. I thought, I used to think, boy, if I ever get out of this fuckin' place, they just better get all the women out of town that day, you know? But you know what I do? I sleep all the time. You were to just leave me alone, I think that's really what I'd do, the way I feel right now at least. Just sleep and sleep and sleep. That's why, this thing, I dunno how it is, what he's got in mind. I admit, he's kind of a crazy bastard. But he's at least got something in mind, you know? I haven't. He come out and the day he come out, he was looking around. And I keep thinking, it's all I do, Jesus, if I could just get some money. I could go out and live like I was a regular human being. But I can't, I haven't come up with anything, no way to get no money. Dean, my brother-in-law, he's not a bad guy, basically, he don't say anything. You know what he does? He reads catalogues. All them catalogues, come inna mail? Son of a bitch, he works, he goes to work at noon, noon till eight-thirty, down the gas station. He comes out, he reads catalogues. Fuckin' electronics catalogues. And she's, he's down there, busting his hump, up to his ass in oil and stuff, she's out fuckin' some guy. So I'm sleeping on his couch and I'm drinking his beer, he don't know me. He's from Malden. Where's he know me from? They got married, I was inna can. But he still, he tells me, 'Look, don't tell Sandy, all right? Because you tell her and she's probably gonna start wondering, how I find this out. But you probably wanna get your ashes hauled, there's this broad I know, she works, her husband thinks she gets off at midnight, I guess. She gets off about ten.' So I say to him, well, I don't tell him, I was inna big hurry for names, Sandy'd be the one I'd ask, he don't need that kind of favor from me. So I just say, I appreciate it. But I haven't got no place to go, where I can take a broad, you know? I haven't got no car. I got less'n thirty bucks. I mean, what am I gonna do?

'So he says,' Frankie said, 'he says him and Sandy'll go out, I can use their place. Yeah, and probably one of the kids isn't gonna get up inna middle of the night and come out, see how come I'm making so much noise, getting laid onna couch. It's not gonna work, and that's it, it just won't work. I got to get some dough and I can't, this thing John's got, it's the only thing I got in front of me right now. I got to listen to the guy.'

'Shit,' Russell said, 'listen to him. I'm willing to listen to him. He just didn't want to say anything in front of me that I could hear. Fuckin' guy, he don't like me. Okay. But I'm not gonna go around and check myself into something I don't even know what I'm getting into or anything. I did that before. I'm not doing that again. This thing I'm doing, I can do that. It's probably gonna take me longer, get what I need from it, but I can do it. I'm picking my own spots from now on. I don't have to sit around and take no shit from the Squirrel.'

'Okay,' Frankie said, 'that's what I'm saying. You can take it or you can leave it alone, and that's fine. I wished I was you. But me, this's at least ten apiece the guy's talking about. You don't want the ten, all right. But I do. And I haven't got no place else to get it. You have.'

'Not that much,' Russell said. 'I'm not gonna get ten out of this. Five, seven's more like it. No ten. You gimme ten and I'll be gone so fast it was like I never was here. I know exactly what I'm gonna do, I get that kind of dough. But, I don't have to get it from what he's gonna, that he's got in mind to do. It's gonna take me a while longer, but I can get it from what I'm doing anyway, and that, that's on balls, see? Balls. It's something I think up myself, how I'm gonna do this. So, the guy don't like me? All right, I still don't have to kiss his ass, I don't want to. Fuck him. So it's up to you and him. It's up to you guys. You want me, you want me in this, I'll come in. He's the guy with the big ideas. Fine. You want to go and get somebody else, also fine. Don't matter to me.'

A blue and white train pulled in from Cambridge. The doors opened. An elderly drunk stood up unsteadily, ignored the doors open behind him and lurched toward the doors open in front of Russell and Frankie. He wore black suit pants and a white dress shirt and a greenish checkered jacket. He had not shaved for several days. There was a large red bruise on his left cheek. His left ear was bloody. His black shoes were open along the welting and his bare bunions protruded. He made it most of the way across the car before the doors shut. He bent, reaching for the curved edge of the orange seat with his left hand. It was bloody at the knuckles. He reeled backward into the seat. The doors shut and the train departed for Dorchester.

'Must've been a pretty good one,' Russell said. 'Like to see the other guy.'

'He fell down,' Frankie said. 'My father used to come home like that. He was a strange bastard. Payday was no trouble at all. He'd get his check and work all day and come home and give the dough to my mother and they'd go out that night, go shopping. And they'd come home and watch TV and he'd maybe have two beers. At the most, two beers. Lots of times you'd come down in the morning and there'd be the glass on the table next to his chair, full of flat old beer. I remember, I tasted it, the first time I tasted it, I thought: how the hell can anybody drink anything that tastes like this. And he'd go to work. But then some times, nothing on the shape-up. Lots of times. And most of them times, he'd come home and read or something. Never talked much. But some times, there wasn't anything, see, you wouldn't know that, he didn't come home, not all the times but some times. And he always, he knew, he knew when he was gonna do it. Because when he didn't come home, when he was late, my mother'd start to get worried and walk around a lot, and when he wasn't there, she's saying Hail Marys and everything, when he wasn't there by seven-thirty she'd go to the cupboard. That's where they kept the money they didn't use onna shopping. In a peanut-butter jar. And if he wasn't there, the jar was always empty. Always. And he'd be gone for at least three days, and when he came home, that's always the way he looked. He always fell down.

'I remember,' Frankie said, 'the last time he's up at the farm. I had to take him up there, and he was, well, it was mostly my mother. She told me: "You're twenty now. You take care of him. I'd do it but I've had enough. You take him up." So I took him up to Drop-kick's. Doctor P. K. Murphy's farm. And I checked him in and he was as bombed as you can get. So, he just had new teeth. And he says to me, well, I knew what he was trying to say to me, he wanted me to take his teeth. Paid two hundred and sixty dollars for his teeth. Now what the fuck was I gonna do with the old man's teeth? I'm probably gonna lose them myself. So I said to the guy, I said, look, he was probably gonna come out of it, one way or the other, they better keep his teeth. And they put them in a box. I saw them do it.

'I go back about a week later,' Frankie said. 'I mean, I liked the old bastard. He never hit anybody. Used to drive him nuts, Sandy's running around the way she did, he couldn't do nothing about it. But, he wasn't a bad guy. So I went up there, go up there and see him.

'They used to sit around in the back room,' Frankie said. 'It looked, they had these tables and a television and it looked just like a fuckin' bar. I dunno, probably they wanted it that way. They got a drink at nine o'clock and one at lunch and one at six, and some of them, Christ, the whole place, the woods're full of bottles. A guy'd decide, he was gonna check himself in, and he would, and before he did it he'd get a couple friends of his and they'd come down every day and put ten nips in the woods where he said. The guy told me, he said there was one guy, he was stoned all the time and he never went near the woods, and they could tell, they could tell when one of them was stiff, and they started watching him, really careful. And when they, he didn't think they were watching them, see, he come up in his car, and he'd go out in the yard and get under the car with a cup or something, he filled up the radiator with vodka before he checked in. They thought he was drinking antifreeze. They always had guys bringing in enema bags full of the stuff. At night they'd go around and look in the tanks of all the hoppers. Guys always used to stash pints in there.

'So I go up there,' Frankie said, 'and the old man's got a buddy. One of the guys he used to work with. They're both on paraldehyde. A little glass of water and the guy comes by every so often and he's got an eyedropper, and a pitcher, and he puts some of the paracki in the glass and some water and they sit there and they sip it, and they, the television's going, they're watching quiz shows or something, they dunno what they're watching, they got cigarettes in their hands and those butts'd burn right down between their knuckles and you could smell their skin burning and you'd tell them and honest to God, that was the first they'd know about it.

You'd tell them and they'd look and they'd say: "Oh, yeah." And take the cigarette out and look at their fingers and then put the fuckin' thing *back*. They couldn't feel nothing.

'The guy's name was Burke,' Frankie said. 'My old man's friend was Burke. They were both on paracki and they both smelled like skunks. Just like skunks. That stuff makes booze smell like perfume. And the old man's complaining. He's been up there a week and he's feeling lots better and he wants his teeth. And the guy can't find his teeth. He goes on and on. Brand-new teeth, guy can't find his teeth, where the fuck's his teeth, now he feels good, he wants to eat, where's the teeth. Burke's asleep in all of this. I think he was asleep. His eyes were closed. I know he wasn't dead.

'I go see the guy,' Frankie said. ' "Look," I say, "my old man wants his teeth. He's in fairly good shape now. Not gonna bite anybody. Where's his teeth?" And the guy tells me, same thing the old man tells me. "I dunno where his teeth are," he says. "I put the damned things inna box, and the box's still there but the teeth're gone. Him and Burke, they been talking about his teeth ever since he come in. I just don't know. I don't find them, I'll buy him new teeth. I can't understand it." '

'So I go back,' Frankie said. 'Burke's awake now, at least his eyes're open, and the old man's all pissed off, talking the best he can without his teeth, "Fine fuckin' place this is, you come in here and they take your teeth, fuckin' bastards," it's all ung, ung, ung, he hasn't got no teeth, and Burke's sitting up straighter and straighter and finally Burke laughs. And he's got two sets of teeth. His own, that're his, and my old man's. Looked like a fuckin' man-eating shark. I thought the old man was gonna kill him. Gets his teeth back, wipes them on his sleeve, puts them in his mouth, I think the old bastard was almost sober. "See?" he says. "See, you

18

little shit? Make something of yourself and stay off the fuckin' booze. See what happens to you? Get out there and make some big money and stay the fuck away from Burke. You cocksucker." Then he's gonna beat up Burke.'

'I tell you,' Frankie said, 'I think he was right. I always thought he was right.'

'You got caught doing it, though,' Russell said, 'that fat little fuck. And now you're gonna go out and get caught again.'

'I didn't meet you at the ball park,' Frankie said. 'Keep that in mind. You're already pushing your luck again, and you could get grabbed too.'

'For what I'm doing?' Russell said.

'Not gonna matter very much,' Frankie said. 'What've they got over you?'

'Year and a half,' Russell said.

'Plus what they give you for doing it,' Frankie said. 'And all the guys, they'll be shitting all over you, stealing dogs, for Christ sake.'

'You know something?' Russell said. 'I bet they wouldn't. I bet they wouldn't even violate me for that. I bet they wouldn't. And Jesus, it's gotta be the easiest thing a guy ever did. This morning there, we go out to Sudbury? Those silly shits. They get up and they come downstairs and they let the dog out. They don't know what they're doing. You sit there, I think you could park right in their yard if you wanted. They wouldn't even see you. They let a four-hundred-dollar animal out, right out the door at you, woof, woof, woof, "Here, boy, here, boy," and you wave a little meat at him. Jumps right in. You tried to go in that house and he was in there, he'd take your fuckin' leg off, probably. But you show him eighty cents' worth of cheap lamb chops and it takes about two minutes and you're on your way. I got this Labrador today, beautiful dog, scoffing down the meat and drooling all over the place before they get the door shut, big tail going whump, whump, whump, happy as a pig in shit because he's eating and he's getting his ears rubbed. That dog loves my ass. You talk about money? It'll be Saturday before those stupid bastards even know he's gone, and I'll sell him in Florida next week for two hundred without even pushing the guy. Don't take no brains. Just the rocks.'

'Two hundred,' Frankie said. 'John's talking about ten apiece.'

'Yeah,' Russell said, 'but he didn't say, he didn't say how we're gonna get it, that he's too chickenshit scared to do it himself so he wants us to do it and he just sits back there and takes his piece without doing nothing. I didn't hear him say nothing about that. He just decided he wanted to get all pissed off because some-body might've used something or maybe was doing something or something.'

'If he says it's there,' Frankie said, 'it's there. And you got to, if the guy's worried about something, well, he doesn't want to go and fuck it up, is all. You can't blame a guy for that. He's all right.'

'Yeah,' Russell said, 'yeah. He's so careful, how much'd you do the last time he got something set up for you? About sixty-eight months, am I right?'

'Five and a half,' Frankie said. 'That wasn't his fault. He did time too, don't forget.'

'Forget nothing,' Russell said. 'He was the guy that set the thing up, wasn't he? And now he's got another bright idea. Okay. But me and Kenny, you give me another week with Kenny and we'll have ourselves about twenty good dogs, and I guarantee you, the coke'll be there and I'll be where the coke is and I'll have the money and I am *on* my fuckin' *way*. One month from today I got a Moto Guzzi and no shit from anybody.'

A silver train pulled in from Cambridge. The red panel on the front read: QUINCY. It blocked the view of the heavyset man as he finished removing the E in SOUTHIE and started on the E in EATS.

'So I guess you're not coming, then,' Frankie said.

'Look,' Russell said, 'go and see the guy. See if you can get him to tell you something about it. I'll be around. You find out what it is, you're still interested, don't matter to me. You decide, you want to do it, it's all right, I'm in. Without knowing. He still wants me out, I'm out. I'm not gonna waste the whole afternoon on it, though. That I'm not gonna do.'

3

'He's getting laid,' Frankie said. 'He said he hadda choice between coming down here and getting laid, and he decided to get laid.'

'Can't blame a guy for that,' Amato said. 'Somebody put one like that up to me today, I probably wouldn't be here myself. So, I assume you're still in for it, who else're we gonna get? You think of somebody?'

'I didn't,' Frankie said. 'I don't know, he's still interested. He didn't, the only reason he didn't come down here, he said if you wanted him to come in on it, okay, he'd come in on it. And if you didn't, okay, no hard feelings, he's doing all right.'

Amato was silent. Then he said: 'Frank, I just don't like the guy, you know? I just don't like him.'

'He's all right,' Frankie said. 'He comes on kind of strong when you first see him, but he's basically all right. And he's very, very stand-up.'

'Which, after the Doctor, we could both use,' Amato said.

'Yeah,' Frankie said. 'I wouldn't mind running into that son of a bitch some time again when I felt good.'

'I don't think you're gonna,' Amato said. 'Nobody's seen the Doctor for a while, the way I get it.'

'That so?' Frankie said. 'I wonder where he could've gone.'

'Well,' Amato said, 'you know, it's hard to say. He was in San Francisco, he was in the service. He was always saying, he'd like to go back there some time. He said it was too cold, it got too cold for him around here.'

'That's probably where he went, then,' Frankie said.

'Yeah,' Amato said. 'Of course, this was Dillon, I get this from. He knows a guy.'

'Oh,' Frankie said.

'Dillon don't look good,' Amato said. 'He don't look good at all. I was in town the other day and I saw him. He looks white, all white around the gills. I didn't say anything to him, but he don't look good at all.'

'Dillon's getting old,' Frankie said.

'We all are,' Amato said. 'Look at me, the way I let that little shitbird of yours get to me the other day? I never would've done that before. I'm yapping at the kids all the time, for Christ sake. For seven years the only time I see the little bastards's once a month or so, and now I'm finally home and I'm giving them hell all the time. I'm always fighting with my wife. I never used to fight with my wife. I used to, she was being a big pain in the ass, I used to kind of roll with the punches, you know? Now I don't. I'm getting old. And I swore, boy, I was in? I swore when I got out I was gonna make every minute count, the rest of my life. You ever get me some place again, I can go to sleep without some asshole shoving his dick through the bars, all right, that's all I ask. And am I doing it? No. Of course I'm not. I'm just as big an asshole now as I was before.'

'Russell'd get to anybody,' Frankie said. 'It's the way he is.'

'Yeah,' Amato said, 'but the way I used to be, I wouldn't've cared if he could piss off everybody inna world, you know? He couldn't piss me off. If he was right for the job, he'd be right for the job. Screw, I'm not gonna marry the guy. All I want, all I would've been thinking about is, is he right for this job, and if I thought he was right, that'd be it.'

'Well,' Frankie said, 'you change your mind or something?'

'I dunno,' Amato said. 'I been asking around about him. You know, not too many guys and all, I don't want it to seem like maybe I had something in mind. That I don't need. But, well, I'm afraid, I'm afraid he's not the kind of guy we oughta have in on this. You go around this thing inna wrong way, you could get somebody hurt, and I don't want that. There's no reason for that, you know? You hit somebody, you're not gonna get any more money or anything. It's just, it don't make no sense. You got to have guys that can, that're not going to go haywire or something, is all.

'These people,' Amato said, 'these're not the kind of people, that're around a bank or something, they *expect* maybe some day a guy or somebody's gonna come in there and try to rob them and, it's not their money, people tell them, how they oughta act. They're not that kinda people at all.'

'Heroes,' Frankie said.

'Heroes,' Amato said. 'They're a different kind of guys, and they're liable, some of them, you never know when one of them's gonna do it, go right off his ass and start making trouble and then you got to fuckin' shoot somebody, for Christ sake. Some of them, they think they're pretty hot shits. Somebody comes in there that's not absolutely cool, well, that they can see right off doesn't know what he's doing and he's not taking no shit off anybody that wants to fuck around with him, well, then it's gonna be different. *Bad,* different.'

'You're not gonna promote that North End thing to me again, are you, John?' Frankie said.

'The barbut?' Amato said. 'Nah, this's different. Although I got to say, I still think you could do that thing if you thought about it long enough and you went in there with the right type of guys, knowing what you're doing. A few guys, some day somebody's gonna knock that thing off, and then he's gonna have a whole lot of money. A whole bunch of money.'

'I wanna meet that guy, afterward,' Frankie said. 'I think probably, I'm ever gonna meet him, I better meet him quick, is what I think. Fuckin' thing. You ever look that thing over? There's a guy on the corner in the phone booth. Funny how come the phone company put that thing right there, huh? And then there's always a guy that's sitting up in the window and looking out at the guy in the phone booth. Coldest night in the year, go down there, that guy's in the phone booth. He's not doing nothing. I think maybe that's how he makes his living. I wouldn't want it, maybe, but it's fuckin' steady's what I think. You wouldn't even think anybody'd go out, and there he is, and then there's that alley and I bet there's not more'n fifteen heavies in that room with the pieces all set to go.'

'There's still a lot of money in there,' Amato said.

'"So much money they lose it, they lose the dice in it some times,"' Frankie said. '"You go in and you get it, they're never gonna be able, report it, no government types chasing you around, you just go down past Billy's Fish and up the stairs and you're set for life." Yeah, and Dillon gets better so fast you wouldn't believe it, I bet, and fifty guys helping him, too. I been hearing about that place since, I think I was about fourteen when I first hear about that place,' Frankie said. 'The thing of it is, all that time, nobody ever did it. I wonder how come.'

'My daughter's fourteen,' Amato said.

'Jesus,' Frankie said. 'It don't seem that long.'

'Yup,' Amato said. 'She's fourteen years old. And the other day, she left her stuff out on the dresser? I see this light blue cardboard thing. I go in and I look. She's onna Pill.'

'No shit,' Frankie said.

'I couldn't fuckin' believe it,' Amato said. 'I said to Connie: "For Christ sake, willya tell me, what's going on here?" So she tells me. "So what? They're all on it." I said to her: "Whaddaya mean, they're all on it? Who're they? What the hell's she doing on it? Tell me that, all right? I don't care about the rest of them." Oh, so that makes me the automatic bastard. "You want, you'd probably rather she gets pregnant or something." I couldn't, I just couldn't believe it, was all. "Connie," I said, "she's *fourteen years old*, for Christ sake. Fourteen. That's kind of early, I think."'

'I think so too,' Frankie said.

'Yeah,' Amato said. 'So, you know what she says to me? She says: "How old's Rosalie when you're going with her?"'

'How old was Rosalie?' Frankie said.

'Eighteen,' Amato said, 'which is a hell of a lot different. Only, of course, I couldn't say that. I always, whenever she asked me, I denied that. And Rosalie wasn't on no Pill then, either. Every month … Ah, she was a lousy lay anyway.'

'She didn't look it,' Frankie said.

'She was, though,' Amato said. 'Shit, getting into Fort Knox would've been easier. More fun, too. I hadda tell her every time, it's true love, all that shit. I hadda be an asshole, do that. And she, she didn't *do* nothing. It was like fuckin' a stump. I used, she also didn't do nothing *about* doing anything. I used to say to her: "Rosalie, for Christ sake, will you get something? You don't want to get pregnant, do you?" And then she'd start crying. It's a mortal sin. I don't know. I didn't. I used to think, I was an asshole, I used to think I really had something there. Now, now I dunno why I did it. It wasn't worth anything near like what I hadda put up with to get it.'

'She was one good-looking broad, though,' Frankie said.

'See the game the other night?' Amato said. 'I did. I was home. Connie finally went to bed. Muscles in her jaw got tired. That's what I like about TV, boy. You can turn off the sound. They had this shot of Snead coming up behind this big Swede center's ass. You see that?'

'I was out,' Frankie said.

'Well,' Amato said, 'I seen Rosalie the other night, I seen her down the Artery. Connie had me stop, get some fuckin' bread. That's another thing, I don't know why it is. I don't ask her, do some of my business. Why the fuck've I gotta stop on the way home and do her business? Anyway, I see Rosalie. She's bigger'n that Swede now, I swear to God.'

'She was a real good-looking girl,' Frankie said.

'Ah,' Amato said, 'she got married. That's what she wanted. That's the thing she used to worry about, I was humping her. I was worried, why the fuck's she such a lousy lay. She was worried, how the fuck's she marry me, I'm married to Connie? I didn't wanna get married again. I got married once. Once's enough for any guy, isn't crazy. But that's what she wanted. She's pregnant now. About her fourth, I guess. That broad? I bet, she's got legs on her now, I bet she couldn't get my pants on, is how big she is. Everything goes to hell if you wait long enough. Connie says to me: "You don't like certain things? Okay. You talk to her, Mister Big Deal Father, that's spending six or seven years in prison while she's growing up. You talk to her. You tell her what a bad girl she is." Of course Connie couldn't've told me, I was in there, what the fuck's going on. How'm I supposed to know it? Shit. There's nothing you can do anyway. It don't matter. It just pisses me off, is all. It pisses me off.'

'Look,' Frankie said, 'I don't mean nothing, all right? I don't care how pissed off you are. You at least got something.'

'Still come up dry, huh?' Amato said.

'You know what I did?' Frankie said. 'I went down the Probation. Like I actually believe all that shit they're always handing out, there, all that stuff. 'Here's something for you. Place in Holbrook needs assemblers. One thirty a week. Four to midnight. Steady work and it'll keep you out of trouble.'

'Beautiful,' Frankie said. 'I'm living in Somerville. How the hell'm I supposed to get to Holbrook in the middle of the afternoon? Never mind, for Christ sake, how the fuck I'm supposed to get home inna middle of the night. "Buy a car. You need a car for your job, we'll help you get your license back."

'With what?' Frankie said. 'I haven't got no money. What am I gonna buy a car with? Why the fuck they think I need a job, I'm living with my sister and everything. So I can keep warm? I haven't got no money, a car. "Maybe you can get a ride," they tell me. Right. Hang around the Square every day, I find somebody that just happens to be going down to Holbrook. Just at the right time, too. Assholes.

' "Move down there," they tell me,' Frankie said. 'Same thing. I still haven't got no money. I had money, I could move down there, I'd move some place else, I wouldn't be bothering them in the first place. Well, they're sorry. That's all they got right now, that they're pretty sure the guy that does the hiring'll take a guy like me. I should probably go down the welfare and get enough dough, I can move out there. The guy's just sick of talking to me. He wants his fuckin' coffee or something. Okay, that's the end of that. Then I see Russell. He's going right along. He'll probably buy a hotel or something in a couple weeks or so.'

'Not on dogs,' Amato said.

'He's just doing that,' Frankie said. 'He's gonna use that to buy something, soon's he gets enough. That's what I'd like to do, I got something in mind like that myself. But first I got to get the money to buy the stuff.'

'What is it?' Amato said.

'There's this guy I know,' Frankie said. 'I see him, he naturally wants to know, how're things going? So we have a couple pops, he's buying, and we talk, and then he says, well, he's gotta go over this place and I can come along if I want, maybe I'll see something.

'So we go down this place,' Frankie said, 'and it's money. All twenties. Beautiful stuff. I had, I could've bought some of that stuff. I hadda thousand on me, I could've bought twenny thousand dollars of that stuff. And I tell you, it's beautiful. You could move it under a floodlight.'

'Better call the guy up,' Amato said. 'Tell him bye-bye. He's gonna get grabbed. He better pass the first one inna drugstore and get himself a new toothbrush. He's gonna need one.'

'John,' Frankie said, 'wrong. This stuff is really good. The paper's good, the ink's good, the colors're right. I tell you. I really looked at that stuff. The guy that made it oughta go take some of it to the government. It's better'n the real stuff.'

'The guy's Chubby Ryan,' Amato said.

'I dunno him,' Frankie said.

'He's not around,' Amato said. 'He's in Atlanta. He's doing ten fuckin' years for that beautiful stuff. That funny? You know something? I agree with you. It's beautiful stuff. It's fuckin' near perfect. But Chubby, Chubby knows a lot about printing and all of that, but, see, Chubby hasn't got no fuckin' brains. Just like your friend, there, Doglover. He's all right. He just don't know anything. Guys like him, the guys you're always hanging around with, well, they're the only guys're stupider'n Chubby. Because all that stuff's good for now, except for wiping your ass on it, it's to sell to guys like you, don't know any better, what's gonna start happening to them when they go out and start moving the stuff. That's why the price's so low.

'You know what's the matter with that stuff?' Amato said. 'I'll tell you. Chubby took it out to fuckin' Wonderland, is what Chubby did. He hasn't got no brains. He thinks, it's good, he's gonna move it all by himself. He's gonna go out the dog track and move the whole run, he's so proud of that funny. So he did. He moved about ten thousand of it, all by himself, one single fuckin' night. Five hundred of them goddamned beautiful things, and every single one of them's got the same goddamned number on it.

'Now of course,' Amato said, 'them guys, run dog tracks, they're all stupid, aren't they? Betcher ass. Dumb as shit. Never occurred to them, race track's a good place to pass funny. No, not on your life. So they never train them tellers, look out for anything like bogus. So of course, them tellers never spot anything, the night Chubby's there, throwing twenties around like he's apeshit and everything, absolutely not. So they only had about nine hundred security guys and some cops and the Secret Service all over the place when Chubby comes back, the eighth race. And you know what he says? They give him his rights and everything, he don't have to say a fuckin' word, and if he didn't know that already, which he should've, he knows now. And they tell him, he's in the shit for counterfeit. And he looks at them and he says: "Jesus Christ. I put them in coffee. They don't look new."

'You know what he did?' Amato said. 'They give him his phone call and he calls Mike. And Mike says, Mike tells him, keep his mouth shut. And Mike goes down there, and, Mike knows everybody. So he goes in, and they're all laughing at him, and he knows it, and he asks: "Why?" And they show him the reports and stuff. And then Mike's gonna go see his client. And he walks inna cell and he looks at him and Chubby says: "Boy, am I ever glad, see you." And you know what Mike says? He looks at him, and he says: "Chubby, this one's for free. Plead it." And he goes out.

'See,' Amato said, 'that's your main problem you got today. You got guys that know how to do things but they don't know nothing about having no fuckin' brains, is all. They haven't got no imagination. The only thing they can think of to do is the first thing they can see that looks good to them. Only, five hundred guys already did it before and *everybody* knows what's going on, so you automatically go out there and you do it and they're watching for you and they get you. You got to think of a different angle, something nobody else thought of for a while, or else you got to go down to Holbrook there and you go to fuckin' work. Everything else's a waste of time, and it's dangerous, too, because you're gonna *do* time.'

'Okay,' Frankie said, 'you're the guy with the angle. Tell me what the angle is. Only, don't tell me, it's the barbut, is all. I'm not going down that alley behind Billy's Fish some night and wind up in Everett with a couple in my head. No fuckin' way. I want dough. I'm not getting dead, gettin' it.'

'How about,' Amato said, 'well, look, let's talk about it. Before we decide. You think Doglover there can handle a card game?'

'Well I mean,' Frankie said, 'shit. Sure, anybody can. They can find one where they can go in and they haven't got to go up against some kind of an arsenal. Those fuckin' things, they just got less money in them'n the barbut's got, is all. Those things're protected. You can't do them unless you're so fuckin' dumb you actually like having everybody going around tryin' to off you.'

'There's one you can do,' Amato said.

'There's ten I can do, John,' Frankie said. 'I know of at least ten of them I can do. But then after, somebody, everybody's gonna have at least eight hot ginzos out looking for me.'

'Uh uh,' Amato said. 'Do this one and they'll, they won't even look for you.'

'Why not?' Frankie said.

'Because the minute it fuckin' happens,' Amato said, 'they're gonna know right off, who it is.'

'For some reason,' Frankie said, 'that don't make me feel better, you know, John?'

'Not us,' Amato said. 'Keep in mind, I know how these guys think. They're not gonna think, they're never even gonna think it might be us or even somebody else. They're pick one guy, right off, and go find him and whack him out and that'll be it. And you and me and that little prick, if that's the guy we get, we cut up about forty, fifty thousand dollars. No fuckin' sweat.'

'I don't know's I go for setting somebody up,' Frankie said.

'You're not setting him up,' Amato said. 'He set himself up. Mark Trattman runs this game. This's the second game Markie's had. The other game got knocked off. Markie did it.'

'Ah,' Frankie said.

'He did it,' Amato said, 'and there was all kinds of shit. One of the guys that got robbed was a doctor, and he had a brother was a state cop, and he was mad as hell, he was gonna do this and he was gonna do that and everybody's running around, they hadda give the guy back about, I dunno, three or four thousand, to shut him up, and they go around and see Trattman. And he puts on this great act. And they believe him.

'So everybody pisses blood for a while,' Amato said, 'the way they always do when the shit hits the fan, and there's about a month or so goes by and everybody, nobody's running any games or anything, and then, I think it was Tommy Balls, somebody says: "Fuck this," and he hires about ten guys to stand around and opens up and nothing happens. So they all look at Testa's game, and nothing still happens, and after a while everybody's open again and everybody's happy.'

'So one night,' Amato said, 'the guys're hanging around and they're talking and all, having a few drinks, and finally one of them says how it's funny, they had that thing and everybody got all jumpy and now they're all running again and nobody's tried it again. Probably having more guys around, huh? Well, Markie starts laughing. See, he can't resist it. So he tells them, he did it himself. He got two guys to come in and he did it himself. The guys got five apiece, they're a couple guys carrying hod that he happens to know or something, and he come out of it with close to thirty.'

'He's lucky they didn't put him to sleep,' Frankie said.

'Well,' Amato said, 'he is. But you got to understand Mark. All the guys like Markie. He's a genuine hot shit. And look when they find out: when everybody's open again. They'd've found out it was him when the games're all closed and everybody's hearing footsteps and nobody's making any money, then, I think, they would've done it to him. But they didn't. And then, when they did, well, what the fuck, huh? It wasn't none of their money and just as long as it doesn't happen again, because all the customers, you're not gonna get them coming in unless they think it's protected, but the protection's really there, well, shit on it.'

'I bet it probably wouldn't happen again that way,' Frankie said.

'And that's the angle,' Amato said.

'What's it good for?' Frankie said.

'I figure,' Amato said, 'I was there twice. I been there twice since I got out. I run into Markie one night, I was in town seeing what's going on and looking around and I run into him and we had a couple drinks and he says, he tells me he's got this thing and I should come up. So, twice, both times onna Wednesday. He runs it two nights a week, Wednesdays and Fridays. Now the guys that're there, that come on Wednesday, there's a few that come both nights but it's really a different group the two nights. There was probably, I would say about forty thousand flying around the nights I was there. There's this one creep that wears fuckin' velvet pants, and he had at least five on him both the nights I was there. So, a little more, a little less. And of course that's just what I saw. Most guys, go to something like that, they'll carry a little more'n what they're gonna let you see, case they get a bad run of cards and they got to ride something out. So you go in there, you're gonna give everybody a nice little massage and everything, you're probably gonna come up with, say, ten more.'

'Not bad,' Frankie said.

'Now there's guys,' Amato said, 'I was there, I heard talk, see, Markie just got divorced again and apparently he had a little party, had a couple hookers come in and eat each other and everybody had a great time and some of these guys're pissed off, he didn't invite them. "Friends only, no customers," he says. So they get on him, and some of the Friday night guys were there and that's how these guys find out about it. "They're good customers," Markie said, "good customers're the same as good friends, my book." So I got an idea, there's more dough there onna Friday'n there is onna Wednesday. So the question is, when're we gonna do it? And I think, I still think, a Wednesday. Friday that place's different. During the week it's pretty quiet, but on Fridays and Saturdays they got a lot of people coming and going, getting laid and all, and that's just another fuckin' thing you got to think about, parties going on and everything. And I think, I dunno, I kind of think maybe there's some guys in there, Fridays, don't come Wednesdays, the kind of guys I don't want to get pissed off. I didn't see nobody there Wednesdays, had any muscle. I think it's better.'

'How're we cutting this?' Frankie said.

'A third,' Amato said. 'I get a third.'

'That's high, John,' Frankie said.

'Not for this,' Amato said. 'I know where it is and I know what it is. A third's right. You, I don't care what you do. You can get that wild man or somebody, do it for five, get him. Fine with me.'

'The guy who goes in with me gets the same's I do,' Frankie said.

'Up to you,' Amato said.

'You're not going in,' Frankie said.

'Uh uh,' Amato said. 'They'd burn me the minute I came inna door. I'm gonna be a long ways away from that place that night and I'm gonna have a lot of people around me, saw me there. See, that's what, that's why I think of you. All I can really do is show somebody where the thing is. I can't go near it, and I need a guy I can trust, somebody that isn't gonna tell me, they come up with thirty, it's really fifty and they're fucking me and there's no way I can check. I gotta just be the guy that does the brainwork on this. What I need's two guys to do the job the way I tell them.'

'All right,' Frankie said, 'I'm in. Now, what about Russell?'

'What about him?' Amato said.

'I'm still thinking, he's gonna be the other guy,' Frankie said. 'You get used to that?'

'I don't give a rat's ass,' Amato said. 'You can go in with Tarzan in his fuckin' spotted jockstrap if you can get him to do it, don't matter to me. I just want, get somebody who's gonna do it right. There's only two things a guy's gotta have, right? He's gotta have balls, which you say the guy's got, and he can't be nobody my padrones know.'

'Well, Jesus,' Frankie said, 'China Tanzi knows me, for Christ sake.'

'China don't count,' Amato said. 'China's in Lewisburg and he's gonna be in Lewisburg for a long time. Making furniture for the government or something, and theres a lot of guys're not too happy with China anyway right now. They think he probably should've got fifteen or twenty in Atlanta like everybody else that was in that thing, instead of just the five. Shit, he hadda record worse'n anybody else's that was in it, and he gets the five and he's not inna same place and, I mean, that's got to make guys wonder, you know? How come? It was going around for a while, China's not even *in* Lewisburg. They got him on ice somewhere, they're feeding him steaks and bringing his family around and talking to him. Well, somebody says it's not true. I dunno. But nobody's listening to China much any more. I already thought of that.'

'Well,' Frankie said, 'I'm gonna ask Russell, then. I don't think he knows anybody.'

'What'd he go in for?' Amato said.

'It was kind of a wild thing, I guess,' Frankie said. 'You know how it is, a guy wants to tell you, he tells you. He didn't tell me. But the way I get it, him and another guy, they decided to go after this drugstore, you know? All-night drugstore. Well, it was one of them guys that the boogeys're always after and he hadda gun in there and there was a whole mess of shit. Started shooting and everything, after they got the stuff, and the guy that was with Russell, well, I dunno. They both had the same kind of guns and I think probably what Russell did, he probably swapped guns. See the guy in the drugstore got hit, but he took the guy that was with Russell out on the way. Anyway, Russell goes on trial and it was the dead guy that got all the shit, put Russell up to it and everything. Russell's just a clown that went along with something he didn't understand and look at his war record and everything. Which I guess was pretty good. So he come out of it a lot better'n he would've, otherwise.'

'You're sure he's not gonna go into this stoned,' Amato said.

'He's not on anything big,' Frankie said. 'You heard the guy. He's a very savvy guy. He knows what he's doing. He knows what it does. He don't take nothing he can't handle.'

'You wanna be sure,' Amato said. 'Guys that go around robbing drugstores, they're not always guys that're just after money. Some times they're hurting and they need something and they haven't got no other way, they can get it. And they need it. A guy like that, he can't live without it, he doesn't get it, you know?'

'Look,' Frankie said, 'Russell's a motorcycle nut. That's all. The first month I knew the guy, all he ever did was piss and moan, he hadda sell this fuckin' monster bike, he had a Munch, one of them Mammoths? He hadda sell the bike, pay his fuckin' lawyer. If there's a bike in this, no, I wouldn't take Russell. He'd go hairy-assed apeshit the minute he came in. The stuff? He uses the stuff. That's all. He's not hooked.'

'Because one thing,' Amato said, 'one thing we really don't need on this is a guy that's going to go in there and start something off and get some guy. Because then they'll have to report it and that's when everybody's inna shit up to his eyeballs. If Markie, Markie did this before. He was gonna do it again, he'd be just as careful as the last time, get some guys that'd go about it in the right way. These guys're his customers. He wants them robbed, not hit. He wants them back again, they get time to think about it and forget it happened.'

'He'll be all right,' Frankie said.

'I hope you're right,' Amato said. 'Now, the other thing is, this thing's gotta move, all right?'

'All right with me,' Frankie said. 'I don't do something pretty soon, I'm gonna have to go back and knock onna gate and say: "Lemme back in. I can't think of nothing and it's starting to get cold."'

'Because it's just a matter of time,' Amato said, 'some other fresh bastard's gonna think of it and then it's gone and we haven't got the money.'

'No trouble,' Frankie said. 'I'm starving and he's got to go some place pretty soon with them dogs, and like I say, I don't get my ass in gear pretty soon, I might as well kiss it good-bye. You got the stuff?'

'A car,' Amato said. 'The kids Connie got, most of them're stupid enough, but there's one of them, probably if he started to get wet and he was outdoors, he'd go inside. I know where there's a nice Chrysler. I think he can get it without hot-wiring his balls. I got two thirty-eights, which oughta be enough. You're gonna have to get your own ski masks or something.'

'I'd like a sawed-off for this one,' Frankie said. 'Something big, scare the shit out of them, you walk in the door.'

'You get one,' Amato said, 'use it. Okay by me. Just don't start taking your fuckin' time about it, is all. We're not the only smart guys in the world.'

4

The 300f did eighty quietly on Route 128 north.

'She looked really great,' Russell said. 'I mean, *really*. Beautiful big tits, fucked like it was going out of style. This's really a great car, isn't it? It's like riding in your fuckin' bedroom, but it's still a great car.'

'I wished,' Frankie said, 'one of the things I really wish, I wish you could still get a car like this.'

'Keep this one,' Russell said.

'Just what I need,' Frankie said, 'a nice, hot car. No, you can't do it, and there's none of them around that're in decent shape enough to buy. Fuck. Tell me about her some more.'

'Wanna blow your mind?' Russell said. 'You're not gettin' any still, are you?'

'Tomorrow night I'm getting some,' Frankie said. 'This goes all right, this's my last night, a priest. Tell me about it. I'll take care my own hog.'

'Well, you had the practice,' Russell said.

'That's nice talk,' Frankie said, 'guy like you that was sticking it in Goat-ass's satchel. Very nice talk.'

'That's the first rule,' Russell said, 'a clean old man. I didn't see no broads around, up there.'

'Who said Goat-ass was clean?' Frankie said.

'Not me,' Russell said. 'That's the next rule. If there's no old man around that's clean, take the dirty one.'

'I should've had them get you a goat,' Frankie said. 'I had some clout with the keepers. I should've done that. The rest of us could've watched. You sure you're not fooling around with them dogs, like John said, right?'

'Dogs're liable to bite,' Russell said. 'I knew a kid, I knew a kid that had a dachshund once ... never mind that. Lemme give you some advice, Frank: stay away from the dogs. You can get nipped, and what I hear, that hurts. Stick with broads. If you can find one.'

'You know?' Frankie said. 'I'm not sure I can. Maybe it's the same thing. Maybe they're not making broads any more, either. You can't get a nice hemi, because it's liable to make somebody sick or something, it burns gas, and it's probably, it wouldn't surprise me, there's no more broads, either.'

'There's broads,' Russell said. 'Just like us. There's always broads. Squirrel wants to do something, he knows where he finds us. We go in and we go out and he's having drinks some place, and he gets the same as we do. He knows where we are. The girls? They're the same. They're just as crazy as we are. It's just one crazy bastard taking advantage of another crazy bastard. That's all it is. That broad I was with? She's crazy. She's beautiful but she's crazy. The way she looks, she didn't have nothing to do with that. She don't have nothing to do with the way her head's fucked up, either. But it is. She's fuckin' batty.

'She lives up onna Hill, right?' Russell said. 'I go up there, she opens the door, she's naked. Right there. Kind of threw me. She is really a good-looking girl. The stuff I been having, well, it's not like I don't appreciate it, you know? I was in a long time. But this kid, she was something. So I stand there, I'm just looking at her. And she says: "We're gonna make it, right? You gonna stand there all day?" So I go in and I bang her. Great. And then we're lying there and I'm playing with her and she had some really good grass and it was great. Except she's fuckin' nuts. The girl's completely nuts.'

'Gimme the number,' Frankie said. 'Don't go back there. I wouldn't want you hanging around with no nutty women. Just gimme the number. I'll go up there and I'll read the fuckin' Bible to her or something.'

'I didn't say I wasn't going back,' Russell said. 'I said she was crazy.'

'I don't think you oughta go back,' Frankie said. 'You're gonna get in trouble, up and coming fellow like yourself, hanging around with crazy people. Turn her over to me. I'll counsel her, is what I'll do. I'll make her feel better.'

'Right,' Russell said, 'and then she'll do what she says she's gonna do and you'll get blamed for it and that'll be the end of you, Cochise. She's gonna kill herself.'

'They all say that,' Frankie said. 'It's the first thing they think of to say, a lot of them. I dunno why they do it. They probably, they went to Catholic school or something. It don't matter. I was going with this girl, I used to go with? Friend of Sandy's. Had her pants glued on, for Christ sake. Not a bad-looking kid. She had kind of buck teeth. Nice ass. She wanted to get married. I didn't know anything, for Christ sake. I wanted to get laid. Get married, go to jail, cut your foot off: I would've done it. I was so fuckin' horny I would've done anything to get laid. I remember, I used to go, can you believe this? I used to go fuckin' *parking* with this broad. I used to take my old man's beat-up car and drive and drive and drive, get some place where she didn't think maybe somebody knew her father'd see us. Used to go down Chickatawbut, the reservoir? I was almost twenny years old and this kid was, what, I dunno, seventeen, probably, and I used to spend fuckin' *hours* tryin' to get my fuckin' bare hand on her fuckin' bare *tit*. I think it took me almost a year. I took her to drive-ins, I took her to dances, I fed her booze, I breathed in her fuckin' ear, and all I could do, I could feel her up from the outside. Through the sweater, through the blouse, if she was really drunk I could get my hand inside and feel her up through the bra. For Christ sake. The night, I finally got my hand inside the bra. *Inside*. I didn't have it unhitched or nothing, just, I got my hand in there. I came in my pants.'

Russell began to laugh.

'I did,' Frankie said. 'And I hadda drive home that way, all stuck together for Christ sake. The guys, I used to hang around down the Howdy. And I'd hear the guys, there's all these broads that put out. And I believed them. And they gimme names. The actual names. And I didn't do nothing. I used to think, this was when I was working the oil company, I was gonna be a repairman, they give you your own little truck and you make about ten grand a year, now, and you always got to go out in a fuckin' blizzard about three o'clock inna morning, oh, it's a great fuckin' life, and I used to think, well, what I thought was, I got to have a girl I can respect.

I don't want none of them whores. You imagine that? True love. True fuckin' love. I don't want no girl that just wants to fuck. I want a girl that just wants to fuck *me,* and you know what we're gonna do? We're gonna get married and we're gonna live happily ever after. That's what we're gonna do.'

'With about nine hundred screamin' kids and a fuckin' house and all that shit,' Russell said.

'Right,' Frankie said. 'So, inna meantime, I dunno, her father wouldn't let her go out with me more'n twice a week. Fridays and Saturdays. I could visit her Wednesdays, but there's always somebody else there and I hadda be out of there by ten, because she hadda go to school the next day.'

'High school?' Russell said.

'High school,' Frankie said. 'I'm twenty years old and here's this broad I'm absolutely out of my mind over, and she's in high school.'

'Some time, I hope,' Russell said, 'you got over being an asshole.'

'I'm not sure,' Frankie said. 'I remember one night I get her home, she hadda be home by eleven-thirty, Friday nights, on Saturdays she can stay out till midnight. I got her home about two in the morning. I dunno if it was a Friday night or a Saturday night. We used to go down the Blue Hills Drive In and she'd French-kiss me and, probably at least one other couple inna car, and it'd drive me fuckin' nuts. Blue fuckin' balls. Three times a week. And I get her home and the old man's up, and he's raring to go. "Did you do it?" he screams at me. I played dumb. "Do what?" You should've seen his face. It's a wonder he didn't have some kind of attack or something. She was standing right there. "*Did you fuck her, you rotten little bastard?*" I was fuckin' stunned. I got my mouth open, I couldn't say nothing. I think I came in my pants that night, too, and I didn't dare look, see if it came through, because once I did, he'd know, and he's still screaming at me. "You think I don't know what you're trying to do, you little prick? You little fucking bastard? You think I don't *know?*" I thought he was gonna fuckin' kill me. And she, that little bitch, she was just as rough on him as she was on me. "*Daddy,*" she says, "your language is *filthy.*" And she stomps upstairs and there're the two of us, looking at each other. He slammed the fuckin' door.'

'After that,' Frankie said, 'after that I can't see her no more on Wednesdays. Only weekends, and Jesus, every time I go there I expect they're gonna put the old man in the car with us, we go out. So, I start hanging around with the wrong type of guys. And I meet a couple guys, and one of them knows Johnny, and I meet Johnny, and I start doing a few things for John. And you know something? I was still in love with that crazy kid. I probably would've married her. I dunno if her old man would've let me fuck her, I *was* married to her. Maybe Fridays and Saturdays. Long's I got her home by midnight. I didn't know what the hell I was doing. Then I got hooked and they try me, I was in the can the whole time, and they all come to the trial, him too, now and then, and I got the time, there. Sandy and my mother and Janice and everything. Ten years. What's ten years? I didn't know what the fuck was going on. I was, I wasn't even twenty-one years old. Somebody says ten years to me. What's that mean? That judge, you know what he said? "If you continue in this path, young man, you'll be in serious trouble before you're through." Then he gives me ten years. Serious trouble. That's probably when they cut your nuts off and make you eat them.

'So they're taking me away, fuckin' old deputy, his uniform's got soup all over it, and they're all crying, my mother's crying, Sandy's crying, Janice's crying, she's havin' fuckin' hysterics. I should've told her, go out and throw the bumper around, always helped me when you wouldn't come across and I sure can't help you now. And the deputy, he wouldn't let them talk to me and I was still punchy, I was on *his* side. I just got ten and I never even got a hand-job off this broad and now I got to go through this? Pissed me off. I said to him: "Get me out of here." And she's gonna do this, she's gonna do that, it was awful. So, I was in about three months, Sandy comes to see me. Janice's married. It don't mean anything.'

'Broads're different now,' Russell said. 'You been in too long. This broad, this broad means it. You can tell. She's gonna do it, and then the guy that's with her when she does it, he's gonna have to explain a lot of things, and that I can't do. You can't do it either. She needs a good leaving-alone.'

'I can make up my own mind,' Frankie said.

'She wouldn't give me a chance, for God's sake,' Russell said. '"We gonna do it again?" Absolutely. Just gimme a minute or so, get it up again. "I can do that," she says, and she blows me. Well, you know, I haven't been out that long. I'm still pretty eager. And, I knew what was gonna happen. But I didn't tell her, and she got herself a pretty good mouthful. Which she kind of gags on, naturally, and she sits up and wipes her mouth off and she looks at me and she says: "Thanks a lot, you bastard." I say, I said, "Look, I didn't know. I mean, you act like you know what you're doing." "Yeah," she says. "Yeah, you probably think I like the taste of come."'

'So I told her,' Russell said, 'Goat-ass always did. Fuckin' guy couldn't get enough of the stuff. Said it kept him young. "I never liked it myself," I tell her, "but he did, and I don't know." So she says: "You turd. You're all turds aren't you, you turd. There isn't one of you that's not a turd." And there's this big song and dance. We're lying there and, it's a really nice apartment, got all these African masks on the wall and everything, and she's bitching and moaning, the first time wasn't any good either, it's never any good, she keeps on hoping, and it turns out, it's not even her place we're in. I thought it was her place. It belongs to this guy she's going with, the stereo, all the rest of it, it's all his. He's in school. He's gonna get himself some kind of thing and then he's gonna do something and it's all gonna take him about a million years or something and she don't get nothing from him, so she calls up guys, put ads in the *Phoenix*, "Ex-con, long dong, love and affection." I mean, she don't say that. But that's what it is. So I say to her: "Cut the shit, all right? You wanna get laid? I come here, get laid. Never mind all this other shit." And she's rubbing me up. And she says: "Well, he thinks he knows everything. And he doesn't think I know anything. So he can treat me any way he wants. But he can't." And then she says, she says she's gonna kill herself. So I look at her, and this girl really means it. Remember the way Greenan looked there, it was all over the place, they're gonna kill him and he was walking around with a board under his shirt, remember the way he looked?'

'He knew it wasn't gonna do any good,' Frankie said.

'And he was right,' Russell said. 'Can't wear no board in the shower. Well this broad, she looked the same way. I mean it. She did. So, Jesus, that's all I need. I gotta tell some fuckin' cop how come I'm inna guy's place, I don't even know, and this girl kills herself and I don't know nothing about it? For something like that they bring back the chair. So I say, well, it can wait, we make it again, right? And we do. And then, after, I'm *gonzo*. That

47

broad's hoopy. I'd, if I was you I'd stay away from that broad, Frankie.'

'I'll think about it,' Frankie said.

'Okay,' Russell said, 'I'll tell her. She's supposed to call me. See, you can't call her there, because the guy's apparently there some times. So she has to call you. She's supposed to call me tomorrow. She was supposed to call me today, actually, only, I was out. Jesus, you should see the thing I got this morning. I got this big black fucker, German shepherd.

'Guy I know,' Russell said, 'calls me. Last night. He's looking over this place in Needham. Guy that owns it's supposed to have a pretty good coin collection. Those medals they're selling now? Made of silver and stuff. "I can get in there like I was getting into bed," he tells me. "The both of them work and they haven't got no kids. But they got this goddamned *dog* in there, looks like a fuckin' wolf or something." So he tells me, I get the dog outa his way, I can have the dog. Plus he'll gimme a fifth, what he gets.'

'So I go over there,' Russell said. 'The house's back from the street and all, lots of trees and stuff. Beautiful. And we go around the back, there's the dog in there, jumping around like he's gonna go out of his mind or something. Barking and everything. "Okay," I say, "let the bastard out." I'm not going inside and tangle ass-holes with that monster. "Let him out?" the guy says. "You must be crazy or something. He'll kill both of us." Well anyway, he racks up the window and that fuckin' dog comes out of there like his ass's on fire. I hadda couple wool shirts on my arm and he makes this whip-ass flying jump at me and knocks me on my ass, but I got the arm up and all he's doing, he's chewing the hell out of them shirts. And I'm, he keeps trying to spit them out and I won't let him. And he's growling like a mad bastard. So, I get this stick

48

in his mouth. Now he's not chewing, ack, ack, ack. Then I put six phenobarbs down his throat and I take the stick out and he's got to swallow and I put the stick back in. He almost bit the fuckin' stick in half, for Christ sake, and I had it way the hell back in there, too. Then, I got this rope, and I tie, I hadda slip knot in it. Tie his mouth shut onna stick. Tie his feet, the guy's helping me. I get him inna car. I had Kenny's car. He's a great dog, boy. If I can ever sell him to somebody, find somebody that wants a dog to kill people with.'

'What'd he get in coins and stuff?' Frankie said.

'Nothing,' Russell said. 'Guy put them inna bank.'

'Bull*shit*,' Frankie said.

'No bullshit,' Russell said, 'I know the guy. He came right around. Showed me what he got. Couple cameras, portable color, some silver stuff. He had the paper the guy got, the guy put the stuff in the bank. Guys borrow money some times. It happens.'

'That's what I oughta do,' Frankie said. 'I oughta go down the bank and borrow myself some money. They probably wouldn't mind, last time I did it I was inna can for doing it, I had a gun.'

Frankie turned the 300F up the Bedford-Carlisle exit ramp on Route 128. At the island he turned left on Route 12 and crossed 128 on the overpass. Beyond 128, Route 12 was dark.

'Once they see what a nice fellow you are now, and all,' Russell said.

'Sure,' Frankie said. 'I can show them my papers, there. Rehabilitated son of a bitch, is what I am. Well, let's see how this turns out, first.'

Frankie took the fifth right beyond the 128 overpass. The Chrysler moved beneath bare, tall oaks. At a slight rise the road bent to the right and a small white sign, in script, said: *INNISHAVEN*. Frankie took the Chrysler right, into the driveway.

'Got a nice golf course here and everything, huh?' Russell said.

'Oh, they got all the nuts,' Frankie said. 'John was telling me, they got a gym and they got one of them saunas and a massage thing. First you get all hot and then you go and get blown off, I guess.'

Frankie drove the Chrysler around the northerly end of the two-story motel into the parking lot at the rear. It was poorly lighted.

'One thing we could do,' Russell said. 'Instead of going in there and everything, we could just wait out here and grab the guys when they come out.'

'Yeah,' Frankie said, 'and get ourselves a lot of Papermates and Zippos off the losers. Fuck that.'

Frankie parked the Chrysler at the front of the driveway, pointing the nose toward the exit. He shut the lights off.

Russell reached into the back seat and came up with a Stop and Shop bag. He took out blue wool ski masks and handed one to Frankie. He pulled the other one over his head. Russell pulled out yellow plastic gardening gloves. He handed a pair to Frankie and put on the other pair.

'Fuckin' things're too thick,' Frankie said.

'Look,' Russell said, 'you take what you can fuckin' get, all right? They got none of that light stuff around. Fat shits're all raking leaves and stuff, this's what they want. Do the best you can. You gonna use the sawed-off or what?'

Russell took a Stevens double-barreled 12-gauge shotgun out of the bag. The barrel had been cut off behind the front end of the stock. The stock was cut off behind the pistol grip. The shotgun was eleven inches long. There were two shells in it. The front of each green shell stuck out a quarter-inch from the sawed-off muzzles.

'Jesus,' Frankie said.

'You said you wanted a sawed-off,' Russell said. 'I told the guy: "Wants a sawed-off." He told me, he hadda sawed-off for me like I never saw. This's it.'

'Them things,' Frankie said. 'What is that, double O?'

'Double O when they got made,' Russell said. 'That's another thing. What they did, they uncrimp the things and pour the buck out and they take them forty-five wad-cutters, you know? Just like the L.A. police. Split them wad-cutters in half, you can get six of them in there. You can clear out a room pretty fast with this thing, I think. You're me?'

'Me,' Frankie said. He took the shotgun.

Russell took a Smith and Wesson thirty-eight from the bag and put it in his belt. He zipped his jacket shut over it. He got out of the car.

Frankie got out of the car and stuck the pistol grip of the shotgun into his belt on the left side. The barrels, silver on the edges where they had been cut, fitted in against his body. He zipped his jacket shut over it. He closed the door of the car.

Frankie and Russell walked at a regular pace across the parking lot. They went to the outside stairs that led to the second deck of the Innishaven. The stairs were wood. Frankie and Russell made very little noise.

On the second deck there was light from the rooms, filtering through blue curtains in even-numbered rooms and orange curtains in odd-numbered rooms. In front of each room there were two aluminum-and-redwood chairs, pushed back against the sills of the picture windows.

'Fourth one,' Frankie whispered.

The jalousied door of Room 26 was slightly ajar. Frankie removed the shotgun from under his jacket. He held the pistol grip in his right hand and what remained of the forestock in his left. He carried the gun at waist level.

Russell took the thirty-eight out of his belt. He smoothed the ski mask at his neck.

Russell kicked the door open and went quickly into the room. Frankie came in fast behind Russell. Frankie kicked the door shut and stepped back against it. Russell stopped at the bureau.

There were three round tables, two beds, a bed table, five lamps, a color television set on a chromium pedestal, sixteen chairs and fourteen men in the room. The men sat motionless at the tables, holding playing cards in their hands. There were piles of red, white and blue chips on the tables. There were four men at one table; five men sat at each of the other two tables. Some of the men had tumblers on the tables in front of them.

Frankie nodded toward the washstand and the door, closed, beside it. Russell walked silently toward the washstand.

A thin man in a red Ban-lon sweater, sitting at the center table, took his White Owl from his mouth and put it in the ashtray. He put his cards down, very carefully, face down. He said: 'Oh oh.'

Frankie shook his head.

The bathroom door opened and Mark Trattman emerged, combing his long gray hair. His head was tilted to the right and he was looking at the aquamarine carpet as he combed. He said: 'Okay, you—'

Russell stuck the barrel of the thirty-eight in his face. Trattman looked up, slowly. The muscles in his face relaxed. He looked beyond Russell and the thirty-eight, into the room. He saw Frankie. 'Uh huh,' Trattman said, 'well, I hope you guys know what you're doing. I'll get it.'

Russell looked at Frankie. Frankie nodded. Russell lowered the thirty-eight. Trattman walked past Russell to the closet and opened the louvered doors. He took two Samsonite attaché cases from the floor of the closet. He backed out of the closet into the room. He turned and walked toward the bed nearest the washstand. He put the cases on the bed. Russell trained the thirty-eight on him as he moved.

'Can I sit down now?' Trattman said. He looked at Russell. Russell looked at Frankie. Frankie nodded. Russell looked back at Trattman. Russell nodded. Trattman sat down on the second bed. He clasped his hands between his legs.

Russell went to the bed. He shifted the thirty-eight to his left hand. He opened each of the cases with his right hand. Each case was full of currency. Russell closed one case. He left the other case open. He straightened up. He stepped back. He nodded to Frankie.

Frankie stepped forward to the table nearest the door. He stopped at the first man. The man wore a light blue turtleneck. He had gray, close-cropped hair. Frankie held the shotgun close to his face; the re-crimped fronts of the shells were next to his eyes. The man said: '*No*.'

Trattman said: 'You guys, don't do that. You guys've *got* all the money.'

Frankie said: 'What you got in your pockets. Put it onna table.'

Trattman said: 'Leave the poor bastard alone.'

Russell moved forward quickly. Frankie stepped back, away from the man in the turtleneck.

'They'll get you for this,' Trattman said.

Russell came up close to Trattman. He touched Trattman on the point of the chin with the thirty-eight. The other men watched. Frankie watched the other men. Russell forced Trattman's head back, by applying pressure with the thirty-eight. Trattman's torso bent in a backward arch as his head went back. He steadied himself by placing his hands flat on the bed. His eyes bulged. He did not speak. When he was rising off the bed, Russell took the thirty-eight back suddenly. Trattman relaxed forward. He said: 'I don't care, they'll—' Russell hit Trattman with the barrel of the thirty-eight, using a chopping motion that caught Trattman at the base of his neck, at the collar. Trattman groaned but succeeded in keeping himself upright on the bed.

Frankie stepped forward. He held the shotgun close to the face of the man in the blue turtleneck. The man leaned forward in the chair. He took out his wallet. He removed currency and put it on the table.

While the man in the blue turtleneck worked, Frankie swung the shotgun to point at the next man. He wore a pale green polo shirt. The man reached for his wallet.

'Now there's two ways of doing this,' Frankie said. 'There's the easy way and there's the hard way. The easy way's for all you guys to just go ahead and start doing what these guys're doing. The hard way's to make us come around and all, which's gonna make me nervous. And, see him?' Frankie gestured toward Russell with the shotgun. 'Me, feeling good, that's a lot like him, nervous. When *I* get nervous, well, you oughta see him, is what I think, but I wouldn't want to. Not if he had the gun. Which he does. Now what we want, we want what you got in your wallets and your shoes and your coats and like that. And them neat little belts that got the zippers on the inside, them, too, what's in them. You can either start putting it out now, or you can sit there and act like you haven't got it in your sock or something. Then after everybody's all through putting out what they wanna put out, me and my nervous friend're gonna go around and make sure. And the guys, the guys that didn't remember everything, we're at least gonna knock their teeth out. How's that, huh?'

None of the men said anything.

'Good,' Frankie said. 'That's the way I feel, too. The less guys that get hurt, the better. So, don't fuck around. Just give it all up and keep quiet and nobody gets hurt. It's only money.'

The rest of the men got out their wallets and put money on the tables. Two men removed loafers, with brass hardware on the insteps, and took money out and put it on the tables. One man, in a blue plaid shirt, removed his belt, opened a zipper compartment on the inside and took out four fifty-dollar bills, folded once in half lengthwise. He put them on the table in front of him.

Frankie returned to the door. Russell moved from table to table, collecting the money. He put the money in the open attaché case. He shut the case. Russell put the thirty-eight in his belt. He picked up one case in each hand. Frankie stepped forward two paces. Russell passed behind him and stood near the door.

'I changed my mind,' Frankie said. 'He's too nervous. He wants to leave. I never fuck with this guy. We're not gonna go over you after all. You been very smart. Stay smart. Nobody's dead. Don't try to follow us.'

Russell opened the door and went out. He walked quickly on the deck to the stairs. He set down the bag in his right hand and used the hand to remove the ski mask. He put the mask in his pocket. He picked up the bag. He went down the stairs quietly, with the two cases.

Frankie moved the shotgun back and forth slowly, covering the room. He waited forty seconds or so. None of the men moved. Frankie stood near the door.

Frankie opened the door quickly, backed through it, shut it and dragged one of the chairs in front of it. He waited.

Frankie stepped back from the door. He put the shotgun under his coat. He moved quickly down the deck. He removed his mask as he went. He went down the stairs quickly and across the parking lot. Russell was in the car. Frankie got in on the driver's side and started the engine. The Chrysler, without lights, traveled quickly and quietly down the drive, under the oaks, into the dark.

5

At five minutes past two in the afternoon the silver Toronado, black vinyl roof, Rhode Island registration 651 RJ, came up Boylston Street and eased into the curb lane in front of a flocked emerald-green-and-white Fleetwood illegally parked in front of the 1776 Pub. The Toronado stopped in front of Brigham's, a car length from the Tremont Street intersection.

Jackie Cogan, in a pilled suede coat, dropped his Salem on the sidewalk, stepped on it, and got into the Toronado. He shut the door. Without looking at the driver he said: 'Hang a right and go a couple blocks.'

The driver wore a light gray, glen plaid suit. He had very long white hair. He put the Hydramatic in gear. 'This isn't near the courthouse, I assume,' he said.

'Nah,' Cogan said. 'Just a big hole. All the construction jocks, that's all there is. There's always three or four of them, sitting in their cars, trying to get warm. Forget it.'

The driver turned the Toronado right on Tremont Street. 'He was very concerned,' he said. 'When I told him I called and Dillon said to see you, he was very concerned. How is the fellow?'

'He's not good,' Cogan said. 'He came in Monday, he was out about three weeks and he came in Monday and he hadda have a guy come in and take over for him. I don't think he was in at all, Tuesday and Wednesday, and then yesterday he called me, the guy he had those days was tied up and could I get somebody. So I did. He's not in today, either. They told, the doctor said if he took things easy, he was inna hospital over two and a half weeks, and then if he took it easy, he oughta be all right this week. So, he's around but he looks shitty, and I saw him, I saw him yesterday. He's still getting it in the arm and he says it makes him nervous, still, not smoking, he'd probably be better off if he was. Says it feels like somebody stuck a knife in his chest.'

'He probably won't be able to handle anything for a while, then,' the driver said. He stopped at the red light at the Kneeland Street intersection.

'He sure can't right now,' Cogan said. 'I think, I personally think the guy's in very bad shape. He was, you know, every time I ever saw the guy he was always bitching about how he felt lousy and everything, his stomach was bothering him and if it wasn't that it was something else. But he's really sick now, and you can tell because he don't say anything about it unless you come right out and ask him, and even then he doesn't really want to talk about it. I think he's worried himself.'

The light changed and the Toronado crossed the intersection

and the driver said: 'He told me, when he heard, that if Dillon wasn't available I was to talk to the fellow he sent.'

'When you get up the movie place there,' Cogan said, 'see that? Go down the right there, and there'll be a place you can park.'

'Is that you?' the driver said.

'Dillon said where you'd be and for me to go there and wait for you,' Cogan said. 'I looked around all right, I didn't see nobody else that might've been there to see you. Did you?'

The driver parked the Toronado behind a pink Thunderbird sedan. 'Mark Trattman's game got hit a couple nights ago,' the driver said.

'I heard that,' Cogan said. 'Somewhere around fifty-three thousand they got?'

'Well,' the driver said, 'probably closer to fifty. Two kids.'

'Yeah,' Cogan said.

'You or Dillon heard anything about two kids?' the driver said.

'You hear lots of things,' Cogan said. 'I heard they had masks on, for one thing.'

'Correct,' the driver said.

'So,' Cogan said, 'maybe they're not kids.'

'They had long hair,' the driver said. 'The people could see it sticking out, from under.'

'Look,' Cogan said, 'my wife's mother's sick and we hadda go over and see her. Sunday, so of course we hadda go to church, too, the old bat doesn't get any wrong ideas. And the priest had long hair, for God's sake. And they could've been wearing wigs or something. You can't tell.'

'Well,' the driver said, 'they were dressed like kids. They had dungarees on and they smelled like *animals,* Trattman said.'

'Trattman said,' Cogan said. 'Look, anyway, there's lots of guys that stink.'

'Trattman also said,' the driver said, 'the one that talked had a voice like a kid.'

'Trattman said,' Cogan said.

'So far's I know,' the driver said, 'there's nothing wrong with Trattman's hearing, or his nose or anything.'

'Nope,' Cogan said. 'Nothing I ever heard about, anyway.'

'But then, of course, when I talked to him …'

'You talked to Trattman?' Cogan said.

'No, of course not,' the driver said. 'Trattman called Cangelisi, and they got word to him and then I talked to him.'

'Oh,' Cogan said.

'Is that important?' the driver said.

'Probably not,' Cogan said. 'I was just wondering, how Trattman decided to call you. I wouldn't've done that.'

'Well, I do talk to him,' the driver said.

'Yeah,' Cogan said, 'but I don't, and I didn't know you, I knew there was somebody, of course, but I never heard of you before in my life. Just seemed funny, is all.'

'Well, I didn't talk to him,' the driver said. 'Trattman. But I talked to him last night and I talked to him again this morning.'

'So nobody,' Cogan said, 'nobody's actually talked to Trattman about this.'

'Just Cangelisi,' the driver said. 'Trattman called him from the place and he couldn't get him and he woke his wife up and everything.'

'Yeah,' Cogan said. 'So all we got right now, to go on, is what Trattman told some guy. And that's what I'm supposed to go out and find two kids on, what Trattman told some guy, I never even talked to.'

'That's not what he said,' the driver said. 'He said that I was to call Dillon, and I called Dillon, and then I talked to him and he told me to talk to the fellow that Dillon sent and see what you thought, I assume it's you, anyway, what you thought ought to be done next.'

'What happened to Zach?' Cogan said.

'I'm not really sure,' the driver said. 'They had some kind of a disagreement. I think it was about the way he handled the petition for cert. Zach. He didn't tell me very much about it, but he did say he couldn't represent him any more. I called Zach when he first called me, naturally.'

'Zach was with him for a long time,' Cogan said. 'I talked to Zach a lot.'

'Not so long, actually,' the driver said. 'About five years. No more'n that. When he first started out he had McGonigle.'

'Magoo?' Cogan said. 'He came up here for a guy and they practically hadda carry him in court in a basket.'

'He's had some bad luck,' the driver said. 'And that was probably before you were born, when he had McGonigle. Then, Zach told me, well, he didn't have as many problems then. That was really before he really needed a lot of legal work done. But then he had Mindich and then he had the fellow from New York, Mendoza, and then he used Zach. "It's good trade," Zach told me. "For five years it's good business. It'll drive you nuts, but the money's good." See, according to Zach, he blames you when things don't come out the way he wants them to, and then he gets a new lawyer.'

'Zach was the guy I had to talk to,' Cogan said. 'Nice guy. He helped me set my thing up. Say hello to Zach for me, you happen to see him.'

'I will,' the driver said. 'Now, what do I tell him?'

'Well,' Cogan said, 'the games're shut down, right?'

'Most of them,' the driver said. 'Somebody called Testa and he said he'd like to see somebody try to come into his operation. So I guess he's still working. The rest of them're pretty much closed.'

'Same thing that happened the last time,' Cogan said.

'It's temporary,' the driver said. 'He told me that. He said as soon as I talked to you, to let the fellows know what you want. Or Dillon, rather. Originally it was to've been Dillon.'

'I talked to Dillon,' Cogan said.

'What does he think?' the driver said.

'Well, the first thing that anybody'd think about in a thing like this,' Cogan said.

'This is the second time,' the driver said. 'That's what he said.'

'It happened before,' Cogan said. 'Four years ago, and now it happened again.'

'The last time, I gather,' the driver said, 'the man who did it actually was Trattman himself.'

'With a couple Indians,' Cogan said. 'He put on a big show and all, but it was Trattman Dillon said he even used to brag about it some times.'

'And nobody found out about it,' the driver said.

'Not till after,' Cogan said.

'Well,' the driver said, 'this time they worked him over a little.'

'Once,' Cogan said. 'They hit him one rap. One. I think, if I was Trattman and I was doing it again, I'd probably get at least one rap myself.'

'Well,' the driver said, 'where do we go from here? What do you think?'

'I don't know enough yet, do much thinking,' Cogan said. 'Because, see, I don't necessarily think this, but it still might've really been two kids this time. Or else it might've been Trattman. But it could've been some guys that knew he did it before. So it's one of two things here. Mark's been spending it a little more lately. He could've decided, do it again, nobody'd ever think he'd do it twice. But, you ever been up that place?'

'No,' the driver said.

'You know something?' Cogan said. 'Nobody's ever been up that place. Nobody but Trattman. It's, it's just not the kind of place that guys go. Except, I was checking around, Dillon mentioned this guy he knew, he used to know, guy was in Walpole and when he come out, they taught him landscaping, and when he come out that's what he did, and Dillon said he thought maybe that guy did some work up there. So I called him. There's eighty-six rooms in that place. It's way the hell off in the woods, and there's eighty-six rooms in it, and except for Markie's game there's not one single thing going on in that place. In the middle of the week the guys that're using those rooms're guys that're selling things, and they work all night. That's all they do. I talked to Gordon and he said he, when the place first opened up, he put a couple his girls in there. "They went nuts," he told me. "All they did all night was sit in the bar all by themselves and drink. The only guy they ever saw was the bartender. They're getting fat and I'm losing dough hand over fist, it was awful." The place moves a little on the weekends, but then it's guys that come in with girls. "Or fuckin' amateurs," Gordon said. "Between the fuckin' amateurs and the fuckin' niggers you can't do squat anyway these days." But during the week?

Forget it. Nothing. There isn't even a regular guy taking action in there, 's how bad it is.

'Now you think about that,' Cogan said, 'and keep in mind, I got absolutely no reason, think the guy's dancing me around. You think about that for a minute. When'd that game go over? Right around midnight, am I right?'

'Around eleven-thirty, I guess,' the driver said.

'Right,' Cogan said. 'They go up there and all, most of the lights're on. "The place does a good business," Gordon tells me, "it's full almost all the time. It just don't do no other business." So these kids, if that's what they are, they go there on the right night and they go to the exact room where it is and they go right in, the door's open, and they take everybody's money. How about that, huh?'

'Trattman admitted that,' the driver said. 'He said he'd started to get careless. Instead of opening the windows or something they'd taken to leaving the door open a little bit, let the smoke out. He said that.'

'Good,' Cogan said. 'But the guy that's running the games isn't supposed to get careless, you know? He's supposed to think about things like that.'

'He was in the toilet when they came in,' the driver said.

'I don't care where he was,' Cogan said. 'He wasn't doing what he was supposed to've been doing, and one way or the other, those two guys knew he wasn't. And they knew he wasn't gonna be, and they knew where to find him.'

'Right,' the driver said.

'So,' Cogan said, 'for now it don't matter, Trattman did it or somebody did it to Trattman.'

'It doesn't?' the driver said.

'Not to Trattman,' Cogan said. 'That's where we got to start. We start with Trattman, and we start real good, too.

'Now wait a minute,' the driver said.

'I'll wait a week if you want,' Cogan said.

'I'll have to talk to him before you go ahead and do, whatever it is you're planning to do,' the driver said.

'Talk to him,' Cogan said. 'I got plenty of things to do. Tell him I said we hadda talk to Trattman and see what he says.'

'He wouldn't object to that,' the driver said.

'*Really* talk to him,' Cogan said. 'You can't do anything else, that I can see.'

'I can tell you right now,' the driver said, 'he's not going to okay anything major just on your suspicions. He's very concerned about starting something that'll make things worse than they already are.'

'I know that,' Cogan said.

'The last time we had somebody handled it was against both our better judgment,' the driver said, 'and as soon as he got better he went straight to the FBI and started telling lies like you wouldn't believe. It's just a good thing for him that the fellow got cold feet when they brought him in to the grand jury. And it cost us a lot of money to make his feet cold, too, I can assure you. So he's not going to want anybody going overboard on this. Who's going to do it, you?'

'Do what?' Cogan said.

'Talk, have this little talk with Trattman,' the driver said.

'Well,' Cogan said, 'I could. But, I talked to Dillon about this and we think, I better not. Might be better if Markie wasn't too interested in me right now.'

'He's going to want to know,' the driver said.

'Sure,' Cogan said. 'Tell him, I talked to Dillon and we think, Steve Caprio and his brother.'

'Dillon knows who they are?' the driver said. 'He's used them before?'

'Dillon knows who they are,' Cogan said. 'I know who they are. Barry was on the *Wasp* with me. He's really kind of an asshole, but he was also, the guy that was the champ had to beat Barry, the light-heavy champ, he hadda beat Barry to get there. Steve's all right. They'll do what you tell them.'

'I mean it, now,' the driver said.

'Oh sure,' Cogan said. 'I know that. You guys always mean it. You gotta mean it. I understand that. I haven't been around much myself, hardly at all, but I talk to a lot of guys and I know. Now, how're we working this? You calling me?'

'I tell you what,' the driver said, 'I'll talk to him and then I'll see what he's got to say, and I'll call Dillon.'

'Okay,' Cogan said. 'Then, I assume, you think Dillon's in good enough shape, he can handle.'

'No,' the driver said. 'You said he can't.'

'Dillon said Dillon can't handle,' Cogan said. 'That's why you're talking to me today.'

'Correct,' the driver said.

'So,' Cogan said, 'that's what I mean. You want Dillon to handle, call Dillon. Okay by me. You want me to handle ...'

'I'll call you,' the driver said.

'I'll call *you*,' Cogan said. 'I'm out, I'm out a lot. I'll get in touch with you.'

6

Steve and Barry Caprio waited together in the doorway of the Hayes Bickford opposite the Lobster Tail on Boylston Street. 'I tell you,' Barry said, 'I wouldn't've recognized the guy.'

'Jackie said that,' Steve said. 'Guy lost some weight and he thinks he's got a wig or something. He's also, he's a pretty sharp dresser now, and he sure didn't used to be.'

'Must've come into a little money or something,' Barry said.

'Probably not,' Steve said, 'not what Jackie thinks, anyway. He thinks all of a sudden, guy started spending a couple dollars now and then. "Probably come outa the divorce better'n he expected," is what Jackie thinks. He used to be the tightest cocksucker you ever saw.'

'Christ sake,' Barry said, 'he hadda be. The way he used to chase broads alla time? What's he been married, about nine times?'

'Dillon thinks three,' Steve said. 'Dillon was there. Jesus, Dillon looks like shit.'

'Dillon'll be all right,' Barry said. 'That prick, he's too mean to die. Ever see his eyes?'

'Not particularly,' Steve said.

'I never saw eyes on a guy like that,' Barry said, 'I never saw eyes like that until after I hit them. The first time I saw that guy, I really thought: He's gonna go over. But he doesn't. It's the way he always looks. Those're bad eyes. He's gonna die.'

'We're all gonna die,' Steve said. 'Trattman's gonna die.'

'Yeah,' Barry said, 'but not tonight, right Steve?'

'I haven't got no inside information,' Steve said. 'I just got a job to do.'

'Don't gimme that,' Barry said, 'I didn't sign up for that. I want you to tell me, Trattman's not gonna go to sleep tonight.'

'Not by us,' Steve said.

'Okay by me,' Barry said.

'He didn't say his prayers or something,' Steve said, 'I can't help that. But we're not doing it.'

'Okay,' Barry said. 'I just wanna be sure.'

'Just what I said,' Steve said. 'Nothing else.'

'Because I always liked Markie,' Barry said.

'Everybody did,' Steve said. 'You, you mostly liked the blonde.'

'What blonde?' Barry said.

'Oh come on,' Steve said, 'the blonde he used to have at the One-Fifteen, remember her?'

'That was the other game,' Barry said.

'The game he knocked over himself,' Steve said.

'We're lucky, he didn't have us there for that one,' Barry said. 'I wouldn't've wanted to be there for that.'

'Oh for Christ sake,' Steve said, 'sometimes you're too fuckin' dumb for fuckin' words, you know that, Barry?'

'Why?' Barry said. 'The game got knocked over. We was there, we either would've hadda do something about it or else we would've been inna shit, we didn't do something about it.'

'Why the fuck you think he didn't have us there?' Steve said.

'That's what I mean,' Barry said. 'That was nice of the guy. He knows he's gonna do something, he lets us out.'

'You dumb fuckin' shit,' Steve said. 'I gotta have a talk with Ma. I know it now, she was fuckin' the milkman. Maybe the milkman's horse. You gotta be the dumbest fuckin' shit on the face of the fuckin' earth. You embarrass me, you know that? You stupid fuckin' ginzo.'

'He did,' Barry said.

'You should've worn a helmet, Barry,' Steve said. 'I mean that. I think you took too many shots inna head. Don't you know why he let us out?'

'He was being a nice guy,' Barry said.

'He didn't wanna pay us,' Steve said. 'If we're there, and we didn't know, he would've had trouble. He didn't want no trouble. He wanted money. He didn't wanna share no dough with us. So he told us not to show up. He's not nice. He's just cheap. Just like everybody else. You dumb shit.'

'I still liked the guy,' Barry said.

'You liked the blonde,' Steve said. 'Come on, Barry.'

'He was married to that girl,' Barry said.

'Jackie don't think so,' Steve said. 'Dillon, either. She was just something he had around.'

'She was a nice girl,' Barry said. 'I did like her.'

'She hadda great big ass,' Steve said. 'That's all you think about, a great big ass.'

'She did,' Barry said. 'Still, not a bad girl at all. Nice bazooms. She was a good kid to talk to.'

'Yeah,' Steve said, 'right. Talk. Remember that night she come out there inna pink pants?'

'Yeah,' Barry said.

'You don't,' Steve said. 'Still, that was the biggest pink thing I ever saw.'

'She was a nice girl,' Barry said.

'You wanna be careful,' Steve said. 'Some night I'll get drunk and I'll call Ginny up and tell her, you're scoutin' strange tail alla time.'

'Steve,' Barry said, 'you know ...'

'I know,' Steve said.

'Ginny's the best thing, ever happened to me,' Barry said. 'I know, you're always telling me, I'm a dumb shit. Okay, I'm a dumb shit. But I know some things. The times that girl, I couldn't count them. You can kid around all you want. I don't care if you are my brother. You know what? I get home tonight, don't matter what time I get home tonight, it's probably gonna be late, Ginny'll be waiting up. We'll have a beer and we'll talk. Anybody gives Ginny a hard time, well, I'm maybe a little outa shape. But nobody better call Ginny and get her thinking something like that, or anything, that, especially that's not true.'

'Oh for Christ sake,' Steve said. 'I was just hacking around.'

'Not on that,' Barry said. 'Ginny, Ginny's sacred to me.'

'Yeah, yeah,' Steve said.

'I mean that,' Barry said. 'The rest of you guys, all right, you can think anything you want. But not me. Not me and Ginny.'

'You mean to tell me,' Steve said, 'Trattman's pink broad, you didn't fuck her?'

'Nah,' Barry said. 'I tell you, she was married to Trattman at the time. You don't fuck somebody else's wife. I wouldn't do that.'

'Jackie don't think so,' Steve said.

'Jackie don't know, is what Jackie does,' Barry said. 'She told me herself.'

'You asked her,' Steve said.

'I didn't ask her if she was married,' Barry said.

'Barry,' Steve said, 'I'm ashamed of you. My own brother, and you asked somebody else's girl to fuck.'

'I did not,' Barry said.

'I'm definitely gonna tell Ginny,' Steve said. 'You'll be lucky, you don't get a mouthful of plates, you come in after this. You goddamned stud.'

'I wasn't married to Ginny then,' Barry said.

'Barry,' Steve said, 'you been married to Ginny since you're twelve, you know that. You just didn't get to church before, is all. Any time Ginny said: "Jump," all you ever said was: "How high?"'

'I did not,' Barry said.

'You did,' Steve said. 'You give up boxing because Ginny didn't want your face wrecked.'

'No, I didn't,' Barry said. 'I give it up because I wasn't no good.'

'Who's the light-heavy champ in Sixty-three?' Steve said.

'All right, all right,' Barry said. 'He wasn't champ for long.'

'Who was he?' Steve said. 'I forget his name.'

'When I fought him he hadda different name,' Barry said.

'Yeah,' Steve said, 'I remember. Tennessee Bobby Walker. Yeah. That's the guy. How long'd you go with him?'

'That was before,' Barry said.

'Not much before,' Steve said. 'Twelve and you TKO-ed him, and then fifteen and he splits you. And, who was that guy on the *Ticonderoga*?'

'You remind me of Jackie,' Barry said.

'I remind you of Ginny,' Steve said.

'He was always at me, like you are,' Barry said. 'That night Walker beat me? He was fulla fuckin' shit, and I was hurt. That bastard cut me onna eye and he kept the laces in it all night.'

'You did the same thing to him, the time before,' Steve said.

'That didn't make it feel better,' Barry said. 'The only thing that bastard's thinking about's how much money he's out. And I was hurt.'

'You should've butted him,' Steve said.

'I tried to,' Barry said. 'Didn't work. He had his head down too low. You know something? That's the thing I liked about Markie. He never saw me fight. All you guys did.'

'And we knew you quit because you're chicken,' Steve said. 'It's all right.'

'I wasn't any good,' Barry said. 'There're guys that're like that, you know.'

'I know,' Steve said.

'No you don't,' Barry said. 'You're just like Jackie. I'm not gonna do this. I haven't got nothing against Markie. I dunno why he didn't stay married, the blonde.'

'Barry,' Steve said, 'they weren't married. That was just something that went on a long time. She was letting you down easy. She didn't wanna fuck you and she didn't wanna hurt your feelings.'

'No,' Barry said, 'maybe, okay, but nothing Markie ever had, went on a long time. He'd just as soon get married as fuck around, he don't care. He's not a bad shit.'

'No,' Steve said, 'he's not. He's just an asshole when it comes to the broads.'

'I still like him,' Barry said.

'So do I,' Steve said. 'I said that to Jackie. I, I don't want to do this, you know? I really didn't. Markie's not a bad shit. I told him, I said: "Look, I used to work for the guy now and then. Me and Barry. Jeez, I don't know. He always treated me all right."'

'Dillon was there too, wasn't he?' Barry said.

'Dillon was there,' Steve said. 'White's a fuckin' sheet, he don't use no breath to say nothin', it's probably his last. There's dogs, I think, not as sick as Dillon.'

'They're both the same,' Barry said. 'They're both pricks.'

'I don't know,' Steve said.

'I do,' Barry said. 'I knew Jackie before I knew Dillon. I didn't work for Dillon, after I worked, after I knew Jackie. Jackie didn't have no work. They're both the same.'

'What difference it make?' Steve said.

'You know Dillon,' Barry said.

'Yeah,' Steve said.

'You know Jackie,' Barry said.

'Yeah,' Steve said.

'You know the way Dillon looks now,' Barry said, 'and it's because he's sick.'

'He don't look right,' Steve said.

'Jackie always looked that way,' Barry said. 'Always. He's got the same eyes.'

'Ahh,' Steve said.

'I mean it,' Barry said. 'I mean it. I did some things for that guy. When the fights're on, and all, you know something? I bet that guy didn't weigh one thirty then, and he wasn't carrying nothing you could see, and you can see things, you know?'

'Yeah,' Steve said.

'A little shit,' Barry said. 'He was always a little shit. And there was a lot of big guys around. And he had dough. And you know something? Nobody ever fucked with him. Nobody. Not officers, nobody. You know why? Because he looked the same way then that Dillon looks now. In the eyes. Like somebody hit him. Only he's not hurt and he's not going down. He's just there. And nobody knew him from the next guy's asshole, then. Now Dillon's sick and he looks the same way. I don't trust that guy.'

'He's all right,' Steve said.

'He's a mean little prick,' Barry said.

'He doesn't act like one,' Steve said. 'He treated me all right. Any questions I had, he treated me all right.'

'What'd you ask him?' Barry said. 'What'd he say?'

'I told him,' Steve said, 'I said: "Look, I kind of like Markie."
He said: "I know it. Everybody does. He's a great guy. I told him once: 'Markie, you ask girls to fuck, you don't even want to fuck.' I said that to him." And you know what he says? Jackie said: '"I'm staying in shape. Besides, how the fuck do I know, I don't wanna fuck the girl, unless I fuck her? So I ask her, and she says, all right, I fuck her and then I know. After."' I think, myself,' Steve said, 'I think the guy's afraid, there's some broad some place inna world that's gonna fuck, and he'll die without asking her. That's what Jackie said. "Guy gets more ass'n a toilet seat."'

'Well,' Barry said, 'that's him all right then. He's got one with about a forty-inch setta boobs on her in there. He practically didn't even get his coat off before he spotted her, and he was right next to her before I could even get a dime inna box to call you. He don't waste any time.'

'He's been at it a long time,' Steve said. 'You know that guy, except for when he first gets married, he goes out every fuckin' night? Every night. When he gets married, for a little while he doesn't. Then pretty soon, he does it again. So naturally, the broads he marries, there's always something that tips them off, they're all lizards themselves and he's not home and they start figuring. But you imagine that? The guy's close to fifty, and he's, he's not married, he's never home. Never. You can say what you want about the guy, he is still one strong bastard.'

'I hope he's quick, too,' Barry said. 'This fuckin' dampness.'

'He'll be out,' Steve said. 'All we got to do is be here and wait, just like whoever the broad is. Markie don't waste no time. He knows what he's doing. Half the gash went into that place, looking to get laid, they ended up inna rack with Markie. And he gives them what they're looking for, too. They all, you know something? They don't even know who he is.'

'How come?' Barry said.

'Onna one-night stand,' Steve said, 'he don't give his right name.'

'Who's he say he is?' Barry said.

'Well,' Steve said, 'he knows us, right? And he knows Dillon and he knows a lot of guys. And then there's some guys he doesn't know, some guys that, he just makes up their names. Depends on how he feels. So the thing is, there's probably four, five broads, come in here or some place else one night all pissed off at their husbands, and they think they fucked us.'

'That cocksucker,' Barry said.

'Hey,' Steve said, 'you got to give the guy credit.'

'Sure,' Barry said, 'and suppose one of them broads that he

fucked and he said he was me, and Ginny finds out, huh? Then I'm deep in the shit and I didn't even do it.'

'Hell, Barry,' Steve said, 'I mean, nobody could recognize you. What's the matter, I thought Ginny trusted you.'

'She does,' Barry said, 'because she knows I don't do that.'

'Well,' Steve said, 'look, he probably didn't say he was you very much anyway. And the girls he meets, they probably don't even hear the name. They're just out to get laid. It's always, he's the head of the fuckin' Mafia. He's got this whole routine he goes through. "Just in town for a couple days. I'm in and out of town a lot." He is, too. Except the nights he runs the game, he's here, he's in Danvers, he's in Lawrence, he's all over the place. Then he pulls out this big roll. He's got himself about eighty fifties there, and it's nothing *but* fifties, either. And he's got the rings. And then pretty soon: "I'm staying with a guy. Can't take no chances onna hotel, you got to sign everything. Can we, can we maybe use your place?" And of course the broad, she hasn't got a place. Well, she's got one, but the old man and the kids're there, and besides, she don't want nobody to know she's from around here. So the next thing you know they're in a hotel and the broad's paying for it. "He can't take them to his place," Dillon told me. "There's no bugs in there, for Christ sake. Bug'd be ashamed to live in that place." But he's got the Cad and the gold rings and he goes around telling broads all kinds of things and they all believe him and he fucks them all. He's done more for the world'n Christmas, you add it all up.'

'Why'd you say that about Danvers?' Barry said.

'Because he goes there,' Steve said. 'There's this club he goes to some times, up in Danvers. He goes over the Beach, too. The guy gets around.'

'Ginny's ma lives in Danvers,' Barry said.

'I doubt he fucked Ginny's ma, Barry,' Steve said. 'You wanna know, though, I'll call her up and ask her for you.'

'Some day I'm gonna break your fuckin' long nose for you, Steve,' Barry said.

Trattman, wearing a mouse-colored, double-breasted overcoat, emerged from the Lobster Tail with a dark-haired woman in her forties. He raised his right arm, using his left hand to guide her toward the curb. An attendant in a snorkel coat pulled up in a tan Coupe de Ville. Trattman opened the passenger door for the woman as the attendant got out on the driver's side. Trattman closed the passenger door and walked around the front of the car. He handed a folded bill to the attendant. The attendant said: 'Thanks,' with no sign of recognition. Trattman got into the Cadillac.

Steve and Barry got into Steve's metallic blue LTD hardtop, black vinyl roof, and shut the doors.

The Coupe de Ville headed east on Boylston Street. It crossed the intersections at Hereford, Gloucester, Fairfield and Exeter streets on green lights. Steve kept the LTD three car lengths back, one lane to the right. He went through the Fairfield and Exeter intersections on yellow lights.

'This isn't a bad car either,' Barry said.

'You ever decide,' Steve said, 'stop fuckin' around and *do* something, you can get something for yourself instead of bitching all the time about how everybody else's got something and you don't.'

'Fuck you,' Barry said. 'Last month I hadda lay out close to two hundred and fifty bucks for the fuckin' dentist. Every time I get a couple bucks ahead, something comes along to fuck it up.'

The Cadillac stopped for a red light at Dartmouth Street.

'I must be gettin' old,' Steve said. 'All my friends're having trouble with their teeth. Jackie was telling me, his wife's all hot and bothered, she's gotta have, what're those things, root canals. "Which is gonna set me back about nine hundred bucks, I suppose, I'm through." I didn't know stuff like that cost so much.'

The light at Dartmouth changed and the Cadillac moved forward. The woman in the Cadillac moved closer to Trattman.

'He's telling her what he's gonna do to her now,' Steve said.

'The thing that really did it to me,' Barry said, 'you know what that son of a bitch whacked me for Maine? Five hundred a day and expenses. I hadda pay him almost thirty-nine hundred dollars. Plus what I hadda give him before, a thousand, take the case in the first place.'

The Cadillac had green lights at Clarendon and Berkeley. The Caprio car went through on yellow.

'That's because you're a stupid shit,' Steve said. 'No asshole inna world would've gone up there the way you did. You, you haven't got no complaint. I think he did all right by you. You had anybody else, you would've gotten hooked again.'

The Cadillac stopped for a red light at Arlington Street.

'I'm not putting the hammer on Mike,' Barry said. 'He's just expensive, is all.'

The light changed and Steve followed the Cadillac, turning right on Arlington Street. A man in a light gray Chesterfield, carrying a briefcase, crossed the street in front of the LTD, walking fast and catching up with a tall albino man who wore a lavender cape lined with red satin, and platform shoes. Steve Caprio changed lanes to the right and closed the distance between the LTD and the Cadillac.

'Looks like he's going down the Envoy,' Steve said. 'Must've got a cheap one this time, gotta pay for it himself. No, I was just saying, ah, it's the same thing. You just fuck around too much. You did something, you could get something. You don't see me or Jackie going up to Maine and being stupid like that, chasing guys around when they're staying with their families and stuff.'

'Well,' Barry said, 'he wasn't gonna pay. He took the dough off of Bloom and then he wasn't gonna pay it back. Bloom hadda get his dough outa the guy. You can't go around letting guys get away with stuff like that.'

The Cadillac moved into the left lane at the Statler Hilton and turned left.

'No, he's not going down the Envoy,' Steve said. 'He's going down the Terrace. She must have some dough after all. Sure, and Bloom gets his dough, and you get, what'd Bloom give you for that shitty thing?'

'Six hundred,' Barry said. 'I needed the dough. Ginny was starting to get the caps, there, and that was the first time I hadda pay.'

'Six hundred,' Steve said. 'So, you only lost about thirty-two, forty-two hundred on it. Bloom give you what Mike cost you?'

'Nope,' Barry said.

The Cadillac went into the Terrace Hotel garage.

'Nope,' Steve said. 'You ask him for it?'

'Nope,' Barry said.

'Sure,' Steve said. He parked the LTD half a block from the garage and turned off the ignition. 'So, you almost go to jail again, and you spent on that what I spent on this car. That's what I mean. Sooner or later you're gonna have to start picking your spots, like I do. Otherwise you're gonna spend the rest of your life tryin' to get out of things that you shouldn't've got into in the first place, and you're never gonna have nothin.'

'Look,' Barry said, 'okay, you got all this talk and shit for me, lemme ask you this: you're doing so good, how come you're still going out and beating guys up, huh?'

'It's not the money,' Steve said. 'You wanna see how much money I got on me, right this minute?' He moved on the seat, reaching for his wallet.

'No,' Barry said.

Steve relaxed. 'I got twenty-one hundred bucks on me right this minute,' he said. 'I don't owe nickel one on this car and I sent Rita's check to her the other day. No, I'm doing a favor for a guy. This thing come up, Jackie's done some things for me when I couldn't do them. ...'

'Jackie don't beat guys up,' Barry said.

'No,' Steve said, 'but there's things that Jackie does do, you know? There's other things inna world that guys do besides going around and doing things to other guys, Barry. You wouldn't know that because the only thing you ever thought about was how you could grab a fast hundred and never mind what you're doing on the long run. Jackie gimme that thing, when he was getting away from the machines he had in the locations on Route 9, there. He didn't have to do that.'

'He couldn't handle it himself, though,' Barry said.

'No, he couldn't,' Steve said. 'But he didn't have to give it to me. He didn't have to say to the guys, "Now, I want you to give this thing to Stevie, he's a good guy." But he did. So, if Jackie asks me to do him a favor, and I can get a fast hundred out of it for my dumb brother, I'm gonna do it.'

'I can use the dough,' Barry said. He lit a Winchester cigar.

'Why're you smoking those fucking things?' Steve said.

'Because they're not gonna kill me as fast,' Barry said.

Steve lit an L&M. 'Well,' he said, 'you inhale them, don't you?'

'Some times I forget and then I do,' Barry said. 'Not very often, though. It's like swallowing fuckin' fire when you do it.'

'Sure,' Steve said, 'and you're not gonna tell me, there isn't more shit in them're these.'

'Shit,' Barry said, 'I mean, how long've we been smoking?'

'I started when I was twelve,' Steve said.

'Okay,' Barry said, 'and I was a big asshole then just like I am now, I did everything you told me to do, so I was eleven. So, I mean, I been smoking close to thirty years, it's probably not gonna make much difference now anyway. Ginny was after me about it, I smoked them Omegas for a while. I did them, and then there was that other kind of thing there.'

'Between the Acts,' Steve said. 'I can't figure them things out, I never could. They smell just like anything else, when you're the guy that's smoking them. But when you're the guy that's with the guy that's smoking them, you'd swear the bastard spent the whole day burning a cat or something.'

'Yeah,' Barry said. 'So, I didn't have any cigarettes for over a year now, except when I was up in Maine, there. I had about twenny packs of Luckies in them three days, I can tell you that. But except for that, I been using these things. I don't feel no better, though. I thought I would. Them guys that're tryin' to put you guys out of business all the time, you think you're gonna feel better if you stop. Ginny told me that too. But I don't. I just eat more. Some day they're gonna say you can't sell the fuckin' things any more. That's what's gonna happen.'

'Never happen,' Steve said. 'Look, how many guys are there, you think, can go back and forth like you do? Huh? Maybe two. They're not gonna do that. Shit, they did the same thing with booze. They do it and, well, look, they think they're taxing them now, right? How much taxes you think me and Jackie pay on that stuff, huh? So you think, they can't get the taxes on what they're letting me sell, you think they're gonna, they're gonna be able to stop me from selling them? I pay on about one third of the stuff I sell. Just enough so it's not too fuckin' easy for them, a kid could catch me doing it. And nobody looks at the bottom of them things. So, and they know I'm doing it, and guys're doing it, and they know they can't stop me and they also know, if they didn't let guys sell them at all, they couldn't do it.'

'Jesus,' Barry said, 'it takes this fucker long enough, don't it?'

'Well,' Steve said, 'you got to allow the guy a certain amount of time, you know. I asked Jackie. I said, "Great, the guy's gonna get laid and I'm gonna wait around all night for Christ sake." Jackie says, no, he don't stay out late. He gets what he wants and then he goes home. Never stays out past one.'

'I still think it's kind of nice of us,' Barry said, 'letting the guy get his rocks off like this. Probably how he stays in so good shape.'

'He's a fairly smart bastard,' Steve said.

'Not tonight he's not gonna be,' Barry said.

'Well,' Steve said, 'I mean, and that's the kind of guy he is too, like about the broads, there. He's not smart enough, he doesn't marry any of them. Some times he's not smart. And the same thing with the games there, see? Most of the time he runs a good game and all, and everybody's happy and that's when he's being smart. He's not making any noise and he's only taking guys that want to get taken and he don't kill it, you know? He don't take them for a lot. And he don't talk about how he's taking them. No, he just sometimes, it seems like every so often he's gotta take everybody for everything, and that's the same thing.'

The Coupe de Ville paused at the garage exit and Steve started the LTD. The Cadillac went down a short street and turned west on Kneeland Street. Steve put the LTD in drive and went east on Kneeland Street. In the rearview mirror of the LTD the taillights of the Cadillac receded into Park Square.

'You're sure he's going home,' Barry said.

'Yup,' Steve said. 'He's just too fuckin' cheap, take the Turnpike.'

Steve kept the LTD in the middle lane on the Massachusetts Turnpike and did not exceed sixty-five miles per hour. The LTD reached the Allston exit in less than seven minutes. Steve threw change into the tollgate basket and turned right on Cambridge Street. At eleven-fifty he parked the LTD beside a hydrant on Sheridan Street in Brighton and shut the ignition off.

'All right,' he said, 'it's the third brick one down there on the left.'

'The one with the yellow Chev,' Barry said.

'The next one,' Steve said.

'No driveway,' Barry said.

'Right,' Steve said. 'Cheap bastard parks on the street.'

At nine minutes past midnight the Cadillac moved slowly by the LTD. Steve and Barry eased down on the seats.

At twenty minutes past twelve the Cadillac moved slowly past the LTD. Steve said: 'If he comes by once more I'm gonna move and give him this place.'

At twelve thirty-five, Trattman walked up Sheridan Street, approaching the LTD from the rear, on the same side of the street. When he got to the rear bumper of the LTD, Steve said: 'Now.'

Barry and Steve got out of the LTD. Barry said: 'Right there.'

Trattman stopped. He frowned. He said: 'You guys, you guys ...'

Steve pointed a thirty-eight Chiefs Special, two-inch barrel, at Trattman. He said: 'Get inna car, Markie.'

Trattman said: 'You, I haven't got no money on me, you guys. I don't, you guys, I haven't got no money or anything.'

Barry said: 'Get inna fuckin' *car*, Markie.' He walked up to Trattman and took him by the right elbow. Trattman resisted slightly. 'The car,' Barry said, 'you got to get inna fuckin' car, Markie. You're *gonna* get inna car and you *know* you're gonna get inna car, so get inna *car*, for Christ sake.'

Trattman walked slowly toward the car. He looked toward Steve. Steve held the revolver steady. Trattman said: 'Steve, you guys, I didn't do nothing.'

Steve said: 'Barry, put him inna back and get in with him'

Barry pushed Trattman slightly. Trattman said: 'I mean it. I didn't do anything.'

Barry said: 'Markie, we're gonna have all kinds of time to talk about things. Just get inna car, all right?'

Trattman bent and entered the car. He got into the back. Steve slid in on the driver's side and shut the door. He turned in the seat and pointed the revolver at Trattman. Barry got in and managed to close the passenger door from the back seat. Steve handed the revolver to Barry. Trattman said: 'Why're you guys doing this?'

Steve started the LTD.

'I could, I could do something, you know,' Trattman said. 'You guys're gonna do something to me, I know some guys and I know the right, I know where to call. You guys oughta think about that.'

'You maybe already did something,' Barry said. 'Maybe that's why you're here, because you did something.'

'I didn't do nothing,' Trattman said.

'Well,' Steve said. 'Then, you're all right, Markie.'

'You got nothing to worry about,' Barry said.

Steve turned the LTD right on Commonwealth Avenue. He

turned left off Commonwealth Avenue onto Chestnut Hill Drive. He took the left fork onto St. Thomas More Drive and the right turn onto Beacon Street.

Trattman said: 'You guys know me. Why're you guys doing something like this? I thought, you're doing all right, Steve, for Christ sake. Why're you doing this?'

'A guy, some guys asked me to talk to you,' Steve said. 'I said I'd talk to you. You know, Markie, talk? Didn't you used to have me and Barry around in case you wanted us to talk to somebody?'

'Sure,' Trattman said. 'That's why I can't understand this, why you guys're doing this to me.'

'Because,' Steve said, 'for the same reason, we used to do things when you wanted us to. Only this time, we're doing it for somebody else.'

Steve took the left at Hammond Street and turned right off Hammond into the parking lot behind the Chestnut Hill shopping center on Route 9. He stopped the LTD in the shadows behind R. H. Stearns'.

Steve got out of the car and unlatched the seatback on the driver's side.

Trattman looked at Barry. Barry pointed the revolver at him. 'Get outa the car, Markie,' he said.

Trattman said: 'Please, you guys, lemme talk this over, all right?'

Steve said: 'Now, Markie.'

Trattman said: 'I didn't *do* nothing.'

Barry moved the revolver closer to Trattman's face. '*Markie*,' he said. 'There's things worse'n talking, you know? Right now all we're supposed to do is talk to you, and that's really all we wanna do. You're liable to get everybody all pissed off, you keep acting like this.'

Trattman hesitated. Steve reached into the car and grabbed the left shoulder of Trattman's coat. He pulled. Trattman's upper torso shifted in Steve's direction. Steve said: 'Markie, you really got to cut this out, all right? You know what can happen to a guy that doesn't wanna do what people tell him. Now don't give us a lot of shit, okay? We're just a couple of guys that've got to talk to you and we're gonna talk to you and you're gonna talk to us, and that's all there is to it. Unless you don't wanna talk or something. Then it's different, you know? You know how things are. Now come outa the fuckin' car before I start to get mad.'

Trattman pulled himself forward and got out of the LTD. Barry got out quickly behind him. Barry handed the revolver to Steve.

Trattman stood next to the car, his arms and hands close to his sides. He faced Steve. 'I didn't do anything, you guys. I dunno what this's all about, and if I did something then I would, wouldn't I? And I really don't. You guys, you guys've gotta believe me.'

'Move around the backa the car, Markie,' Steve said.

Trattman raised his hands slightly, palms up.

'*Move*, Markie, you fuckin' little prick,' Steve said. 'You tryin' to make me shoot you, for Christ sake?'

Trattman moved sideways to the left rear panel of the LTD. He stood with his arms tight against his sides. Steve stood three feet away from him, pointing the revolver. Barry walked around behind Steve and stood at his right.

'Honest to God,' Trattman said, 'Steve, may my mother get cancer, I had nothing to do with it. Honest to God, Steve. You, can't you tell them that? I know how it looks. I know. But honest to God, Steve, I didn't.'

'He didn't do it,' Barry said. 'That what you were gonna ask him, Steve?'

'Yeah,' Steve said.

'That's what we're supposed to talk to you about, Markie,' Barry said.

'Yeah,' Steve said, 'this thing, you didn't have nothing to do with it?'

'Steve,' Trattman said.

'What thing was that, Markie?' Steve said.

'Steve,' Trattman said. His voice broke. 'Steve, did I ever lie to you? I never told you anything, did I?'

'Now?' Barry said.

'Uh huh,' Steve said.

Barry took two strides toward Trattman, closing his right hand and swinging the fist back in the motion of a softball pitcher. Trattman jerked his hands up toward his face. Barry swung his fist forward and punched Trattman in the groin as Trattman's torso began to move backward over the trunk of the LTD. When the fist connected, Trattman's torso stopped and began to move forward quickly. His hands dropped from his face. His mouth gaped. His eyes stared. He exhaled and moaned simultaneously. He clapped his hands to his groin. He doubled over.

Barry took a short stride backward. He stepped forward on his left foot and brought his right knee up fast. It caught Trattman on the mouth. There was a cracking sound. Trattman's head snapped up. His body, still in a crouch, sagged off to the left.

Barry grabbed the lapels of Trattman's coat and pulled him up. He leaned Trattman against the car. Trattman kept his head down. He cried. He spit blood and pink material from his mouth. He raised his head. He had closed his eyes. His nose and mouth were pulpy and covered with blood. Some blood and pink material were on his coat.

'What's this thing you didn't have nothing to do with, Markie?' Steve said.

Trattman moved his head once to the left and once to the right. He extended his tongue, then retracted it, tracing the tip of it along his lips. He lowered his head and spat blood and pink material on the pavement of the parking lot.

'He don't answer,' Barry said.

'Must be there's nobody home or something,' Steve said.

'Maybe I better knock again,' Barry said. 'Make sure.'

'Yeah,' Steve said.

'*No*,' Trattman said, uttering it in a high voice as 'Mo.'

'Shut up, you fuck,' Barry said. He hit Trattman very hard, twice, in the pit of the stomach. Trattman started to double over with the impact of the first punch. The second brought a rush of air from his mouth. Steve and Barry stepped back two paces, quickly. Trattman fell forward on the pavement and vomited half-digested steak and salad, and blood. He lay on his chest, his head resting on its left side. He breathed noisily.

'Whaddaya think, Steve,' Barry said, 'you think he's through?'

'Better give him another minute or so,' Steve said. 'He might have some more in him.'

Trattman, his eyes closed, expelled more vomit, blood and pink material from his mouth. It ran down his cheek to the pavement.

'Give him a try now,' Steve said.

Barry stepped forward. He picked Trattman up by the collar of his coat, at the nape of the neck. He leaned Trattman against the side of the LTD. Trattman's head lolled off to the left. His eyes remained closed.

'Who're the kids, Markie?' Steve said.

Trattman retched and bled from the mouth and nose. He raised his right hand feebly toward his face. He touched his face lightly with the tips of his fingers. Slowly he shook his head.

'Can't hear you, Markie,' Steve said. 'Who're the kids, Markie?'

Trattman explored the pulpy flesh around his mouth. He sighed. Tears came from his closed eyes. He shook his head slowly. 'I,' he said, 'they ... I didn't ...'

'He still says he don't know nothing,' Barry said.

'Yeah,' Steve said, 'how about that?'

'Think he doesn't?' Barry said.

'Jesus,' Steve said, 'maybe he doesn't, after all.'

'You can't tell about guys, though,' Barry said.

'I know it,' Steve said. 'I heard about a guy once, somebody asked him if he knew a couple guys and he said he didn't. But you know what? He did.'

'Better ask him again?' Barry said.

'Yeah,' Steve said.

Trattman screamed softly through his bloody lips.

'Pick a place,' Steve said, 'you don't get all covered with stuff.'

Trattman moaned. His head lolled to the right. He got his eyes open as Barry stepped forward again. He saw Barry's right hand, closed in a fist, swing back across Barry's chest until the fist passed over Barry's left shoulder. He closed his eyes quickly and moved, jerkily, to his own left. Barry brought his fist back in a flat arc. The heel of his hand hit Trattman at the right hinge of his jaw. His head snapped fast to the left as the bone broke. His torso stretched upward and to the left, then sagged down. The back of his head hit the edge on the left rear fender of the LTD. When he hit the pavement he was lying on his left side, face up. His eyelids fluttered open, then closed. He gagged softly on something wet in his throat.

Steve walked up to Trattman and bent over him. 'Markie,' he said softly, 'you sure?'

Trattman moaned. His head shifted on the pavement.

'About the kids,' Steve said. 'It's the kids, Markie, we're supposed to talk to you about. You sure you don't know who those kids are? You really sure?'

Trattman moved his head slightly.

'Because I got to be sure,' Steve said. 'I really got to be, Markie, that's all there is to it. You make me stay here all night, me and Barry, making sure, I'm not gonna like it. And it's gonna be an awful long night for you, Markie.'

Trattman vomited suddenly, a small amount of pink material and blood. Some of it spattered Steve's shoes and the wide cuffs of his pants.

'You bastard,' Steve said. He stepped back quickly. He stepped forward quickly and kicked Trattman on the left side of the rib cage, near the belt. Ribs cracked. Holding his foot at an angle, Steve wiped his shoe on the skirt of Trattman's coat. Trattman gasped and moaned and sighed. 'You cocksucker,' Steve said. He stepped back again.

'Whaddaya think, Steve?' Barry said.

'Get inna car,' Steve said. 'Strikes me right, I'll back over the prick.'

As the LTD began to move, the taillights illuminated Trattman in red. Then he lay in the mist and darkness, breathing loudly and moaning from time to time. Then he passed out.

The LTD left the parking lot at the Hammond Pond Parkway exit.

On Route 9, eastbound, Barry said: 'I hurt my fuckin' hand again. I always do.'

'Kiss it and make it better,' Steve said. 'It'll be all right. That fuckin' Cogan, though. I'm gonna make him pay for these clothes that that cocksucker ruined.'

'Think we oughta get the car washed?' Barry said.

'I'm gonna,' Steve said. 'Just be onna safe side. I'm gonna leave you off, and you take the gun, okay? There's a place in Watertown, it's open all night. I'll go there.'

'And then,' Barry said, 'then where're you gonna go?'

'None of your fuckin' business,' Steve said. 'Why, you wanna come?'

'I'm not gonna be able to sleep,' Barry said. 'I always have to calm down some.'

'Tell Ginny you don't want no beer,' Steve said. 'Have her give you some warm milk and stuff.'

'Fuck you,' Barry said. 'Whaddaya think, though, about the guy? Think he knows?'

'I don't think,' Steve said. 'Who the fuck wants to think about him? He's just a shit.'

'Well,' Barry said, 'I mean, I worked him over pretty good.'

'Probably,' Steve said, 'he probably knows.'

'He stood up pretty good, then,' Barry said. 'If he does, I mean.'

'He's gotta stand up pretty good,' Steve said. 'He knows what's gonna happen to him, he doesn't. He knows.'

7

Frankie parked the dark green GTO convertible in front of Amato's Driving School and got out. He wore tan flared corduroy jeans over Dingo boots, a white turtleneck and a doubleknit gray blazer. He locked the car and went inside.

'Well,' Amato said, 'you still got a good ways to go, but you look a little better, anyway. And the hair's a lot better. You got too much of that spray on it there, though.'

'I don't spray it,' Frankie said. 'I ain't no fuckin' queer. That's gel on it. The guy that cut it gave me the stuff.'

'Find another guy, the next time,' Amato said. 'Also got yourself something to drive around in, I see.'

'I was never that hot for trolleys,' Frankie said.

'What'd it go for?' Amato said.

'Eighteen hundred,' Frankie said. 'Plus the fuckin' sales tax, of course. It's in pretty good shape.'

'Things're a little better,' Amato said.

'Things're a lot better,' Frankie said. 'I was out last night, me this girl, I had a place to take her and a car to take her to the place in. I got that thing? I had a little beef with the guy down to Probation, there. Can't understand it, I got to have my license back so soon. So I hadda tell my brother-in-law, I went back to get my stuff. "By the way, anybody asks you, you loaned me the money, all right?" So he looks at it. Dean's all right. "I'm not asking no questions," he says, "nothing like that at all. But I think you're doing better'n me, all of a sudden." Yeah, it's really great. I was down the Probation and the guy looks at me and he says: "Nice clothes." I said: "Look, the last time I come in, you're giving me the hardeyes, I look like a bum. I figured you're gonna violate me for it, for Christ sake. So now I beat up on my family and get some dough and I finally look like something that didn't come in on a truckload of chickens, and now you're pissed about that." Yeah, it's great.'

'Where're you living?' Amato said.

'Place in Norwood,' Frankie said. 'Just a studio thing, the furniture was all in it. It's right on Route 1, though. But what the fuck if it's noisy, you know? The noise's all outside.'

'The fuck'd you go all the way out there for,' Amato said. 'I would've thought, guy like you'd stay around Boston some place. I would.'

'Well,' Frankie said, 'it's a little cheaper, you know? And, I know too many guys around right in town. My brother-in-law, for example, I hadda place in Boston, the first thing you know he'd want to be coming over all the time and using the place, and then Sandy'd get all pissed off at me and everything. And, I just thought about it and I figured, it's gonna be more of a hassle living there'n it's gonna be of a hassle to live some place else. The guy down Probation, he got all stirred up about that, too. 'How come you're in Norwood? What're you doing there?' So I told him, guy I know's gonna give me a job there, how's that? Taking care of the building, and I get something off of my rent and everything and I can still get another job and stay out of trouble.'

'They check on that,' Amato said. 'That's one thing they do check on.'

'And when they do,' Frankie said, 'they're gonna call the guy and that's exactly what he's gonna tell them. I'm a maintenance engineer for Hes-Lee Apartments.'

'Janitor,' Amato said.

'Janitor,' Frankie said.

'What's that pay?' Amato said.

'Well,' Frankie said, 'it pays fifty, sixty a week. Only I don't think I probably oughta try and collect it very often, you know? The guy's, I told him I just got out of the can, and pretty soon I'm in talking to the head honcho, this big enormous Jew. It was his idea.'

'He's fuckin' around with his taxes,' Amato said.

'Yeah,' Frankie said, 'or he's got a honey some place or something. I dunno. I don't give a shit.'

'So,' Amato said, 'what *are* you gonna do, then?'

'Well,' Frankie said, 'that's one of the things I come down, I figured I'd talk to you about, you know? See, I was thinking about some things and I was talking to Russell about some things and he was thinking about some things, but I didn't want to do anything, really, until we see. If things come out all right on that other thing. So, I hear, I hear they did. And I come down.'

'Trattman got the shit beaten out of him,' Amato said.

'That's what I mean,' Frankie said. 'So I was wondering, you got anything else in mind?'

'No,' Amato said, 'I really don't. You know how I know I don't? I stop down the Square in the morning. I go in, get the paper, see a couple the guys, maybe there's something going on. I always did that, before, and the minute I get out, I'm doing it again. I'm like them old guys you see, the first thing they do in the morning's go down and stand up at the bar and have coffee and anisette. Except I don't have no coffee or anything, and instead I get a newspaper. It's just a habit. And, I been doing this for a long time, I always seen the Brink's, every Friday morning. Picking up the dough for the Armstrong factory. Since I was, what, since I was fifteen, probably. I used to do that when I was going to school. I played the dogs something fierce when I was in school.'

'Uh uh,' Frankie said.

'Well,' Amato said, 'that's what I mean. How I know, I really haven't got anything. Because when I start thinking about that, I'm not thinking any more. Outside the barbut, no, nothing.'

'I still feel the same way about that,' Frankie said. 'I personally don't think anybody could get past Billy's Fish before you had guys all over you. And that alley, that alley's narrow. I bet it isn't more'n three feet wide.'

'You went down there again, huh?' Amato said.

'I was down there the night, the night before last,' Frankie said. 'I heard about Trattman. So, I wouldn't want to've been Trattman or anything, but I didn't feel *bad* about it, you know? Come out just like you said. I can't just sit around now. I got to get something else lined up. I was thinking, you know? And one of the things, the way guys get back in, they do something, and they plan it right and everything, and they do it and it works. And then they sit around. And then they run outa dough. And then they got to do something else, quick. And they do. And they get caught and they go away again. I don't want to do that. I'm not doing no more time.

'I start thinking,' Frankie said. '"John's right about the other thing, I'm right down here, maybe he's right about this." So I went over and I looked it over. Of course this wasn't, I think it was Tuesday or something and there wasn't anybody standing around watching everybody, you know? So that'd be different. But, I still don't think it makes much difference, John. I still don't think you can touch that thing.'

'You're probably right,' Amato said. 'That's another habit I got. See, at least I know it. When I can't think of anything I start thinking about that or the Brink's again. I'd like to do that one, you know? It's the kind of thing, it's almost like a sitting duck, except it isn't. Both of them are. Plus which, there's a lot of dough in both of them. And I can always use some of that.'

'You haven't been doing good again?' Frankie said.

'Frank,' Amato said, 'I been getting *murdered,* is what I been doing. I dunno what the fuck it is. I'm not stupid. It seems like, the last good year I had was, you know when that was? I was thinking about it. It was nineteen sixty-two, can you imagine that? I got nothing in sixty-three, nothing. I think I was lucky if I even broke even. And I was getting my *balls* cut off when we did that thing. That's why I went for it, for Christ sake. That's what started making me think about it in the first place.'

'That's one of the things I was thinking about,' Frankie said, 'another one of those.'

'Jesus, Frank,' Amato said, 'I don't know. Those guys, knocked over the South Shore the other day? Buncha fuckers, I dunno who they were. I had about six cops walking up and down out front here, waiting around, see if anybody's gonna come around and see me. They're gonna be thinking about us now, anything like that happens.'

'Let 'em think,' Frankie said. 'I was thinking, the thing that went ragtime the last time, it was Mattie.'

'Right,' Amato said.

'We had somebody instead of Mattie, that didn't shit a fuckin' brick when somebody asks him his name or something,' Frankie said, 'we wouldn't've had no problem at all.'

'That's right,' Amato said. 'Shit, the first time, there, even the Doctor was all right. He must've had the fuckin' rag on or something.'

'All right,' Frankie said. 'And another thing was, we had, I think we probably had too many guys. That's another thing I was thinking about. I think, two guys working oughta be enough. One that's gonna set everything up and then the two guys that never went *near* the place, to actually do it, and then, you keep it down to that many guys, you oughta be able, kind of control the kind of guys you get, you know?'

'We couldn't do it around here,' Amato said.

'I wasn't thinking of around here,' Frankie said. 'What I was thinking, how about down around Taunton some place? How about that?'

'Too hard,' Amato said. 'I couldn't get down there that often. For Christ sake, I take half a day off or something, go over the Registry and take care a lot of fuckin' horseshit oughta take about ten minutes, I got to talk to a lot of fuckin' stooges that haven't got no manners, it takes me half a day? You know something? I haven't got no real complaint. A guy gets himself elected to something

97

or something, he's got a whole family full of morons, they can't get no work humping the garbage? Beautiful. I'd rather, they're doing something, they're doing nothing and we're all carrying the lazy fuckers onna welfare. But these people, they haven't got no *manners*. I can tell you what they are, you know what they are? They're, they don't give a shit. You can stand there and stand there and stand there, of course you haven't got nothing else to do, and then, they're all sitting around, these young cunts with big tits and everything, and it gets to be four-thirty, they just sit down. They go talk to their boyfriends, about how they're gonna do it inna fuckin' bathtub or something that night, and then it's five o'clock and they hang up, he's running the fuckin' water or something, and they tell you, come back tomorrow. Fuck you, in other words.

'I got the same problem here,' Amato said. 'Nobody's doing a fuckin' thing. I go down the Registry, I stand around all the time there, I waste the whole fuckin' day, I come back here, you think anybody's doing anything? Wrong. They're all fuckin' around. Talking, bullshittin' and everything. Connie, I give Connie credit. She did the best she could with this thing. I admit it. I come back and it's still running, which I didn't expect. But it's just all right. The kids she got in here, they'll work if you watch them like hawks. But you just let them find out you're not gonna be around for a day or so and watch them goof off. It's something awful.

'Last month?' Amato said. 'Last month the bills're almost a week late going out. The checks're two and a half, at least. I had guys calling me up. "Uh, Mister Amato, about your order?" And then he tells me, three new transmissions he put in, couple tune-ups, I also owe for three tires they hadda have fixed, one of my great customers don't know they got curbs on roads, and the guy's into me for around eight hundred bucks and he wouldn't mind seeing his money.'

'So I go out there,' Amato said, 'the kid's sitting there. She's putting on nail polish, for Christ sake, she's talking to her boyfriend onna phone. I wait. I only pay her, for Christ sake. No reason she oughta stop talking about how they're gonna do it after closing, it's not closing yet and I'm still paying her. No, of course not. She finally gets off. I tell her, Jesus Christ, we can't do business like this. We need a wrecker or something, this guy, he's not gonna send one. "*Mister* Amato," she says, "I haven't had *time.* I've been so *busy.*" Jesus. I pay that broad one thirty-five for that.'

'That the one with the nice ass?' Frankie said.

'That's the one,' Amato said. 'Before I get through that silly little bitch's gonna have me in court, and I'm gonna look awful stupid, I'm telling the judge, I got the money, I just couldn't get the girl to hang up long enough to send it out.'

'How is she?' Frankie said.

Amato did not reply immediately. Then he said: 'Well, okay, yeah. But Jesus Christ, I mean, you still gotta get the work done and everything.'

'You don't learn nothing,' Frankie said. He was grinning. 'I bet when you were a little kid it took them about eight years to get you to stop shitting in your pants.'

'I know it,' Amato said. 'But, I still can't be going down to Taunton or some place every day. I got to keep this thing going even if I can't do anything else, you know?'

'Every day,' Frankie said, 'that'd be if you're going in when it's open.'

'You wanna go in through the roof or something?' Amato said.

'Yeah,' Frankie said. 'One of them Sunday night jobs. The back wall or something like that. Two guys that knew where everything was, and I figure, somebody went down there once and just made a little map, that'd be enough to go in on. You know what you're gonna have to do when you get in there. All you got to know is where it is.'

'You'd have to get a guy, knew bells and stuff,' Amato said. 'Doglover know anything about bells?'

'I wasn't thinking about Russell,' Frankie said. 'If I was gonna go in when it's open again, I'd get Russell. But anyway, Russell took off. Him and the guy he's stealing the dogs with. I dunno if he's gonna be back and if he was, he probably wouldn't want to do it. He's gonna deal.'

'What's he got?' Amato said.

'I didn't really ask him,' Frankie said. 'Coke, I think.'

'He's gonna make a million bucks off of that,' Amato said.

'He might,' Frankie said, 'and he might just get himself grabbed about six minutes after he starts and then *do* twenty more. That stuff's dangerous. There isn't anything around, you know? Everybody's hunting around and half of them're narcs. I heard a couple guys, they got sixty thousand hits of meth off a terminal down in Pawtucket, and they come back up, these're tough guys, and about ten freaks ripped them off. The cops've got bigger hardons for that'n they got for fuckin' coons with fuckin' guns, for Christ sake. Russell's got balls, but he didn't ask me and I don't think this guy he's working the dogs with, I don't think he's in it with him. I don't think anybody's in it with him, which is no way to be if you're gonna do something like that. No, I was thinking, Dean, my brother-in-law. When he was in the service he was Electronics SP, and he still fools around with that stuff all the time.'

'Alarms?' Amato said. 'I thought the guy works in a gas station.'

'He does,' Frankie said. 'No, but he built one of them quadraphonic things from a kit on the table in the kitchen, and he was telling me, well, when he saw my car? "Now if I was to get that, if I ever got myself a few extra bucks," he tells me, he'd build his own color television. It's all the same thing, isn't it? I mean, it's just circuits and stuff, and he knows about that.'

'You think he'd go for it?' Amato said.

'I won't know till I ask him,' Frankie said. 'See, I wanted, talk to you, first, see what you thought about it. I can't lay the place out like you can. I'm all right going in, but I got to have the map in front of me. I don't notice things like you do. So, I wanted, talk to you, first. Before I see him. I think he will, though, yeah.'

'He ever do anything before?' Amato said.

'I think he did favors for a couple guys that bought cars,' Frankie said. 'And he told me, mine needs a tune-up or something, he'll do it for me and the parts aren't gonna cost me anything. He's hurtin' for dough.'

'Has it got to be Taunton?' Amato said.

'Shit, no,' Frankie said. 'I just said that, account of the way everybody's so interested in what we do around here. I haven't got no particular one in mind. What I want, I want the easiest one around to get into, probably one of those new ones that they made outa plastic or something, and that's got some money in it, and maybe some other things around it so you're not bare-ass to the world when you're doing it.'

'I took Connie the movies the other night,' Amato said. 'Some fuckin' thing, and it's over in Brockton there, in this shopping plaza they got. It's, I dunno what the name of it is. One story.'

'How about,' Frankie said, 'take a look at it, and I'll go drive past it too, and then if it looks good we can start thinking about it.'

'Yeah,' Amato said. 'Yeah, I'm beginning to like this, you know? It's funny about a thing, like that last thing, there, you can tell right off, if it feels right.'

8

'He's an asshole,' Cogan said. He sat in the silver Toronado. It was parked in the MBTA lot behind Cronin's in Cambridge. 'The *way* he's an asshole, he's a gambler. He thinks he's a gambler, at least. What he really is is a jerk. He don't gamble, he *bets* on everything. Jerk of the year.'

'I enjoy going to the track now and then myself,' the driver said. 'I haven't missed an opening at Lincoln in years.'

'So do I,' Cogan said. 'I still do. Even though, every time I go down the track, I lose.'

'I don't,' the driver said. 'Of course I don't bet very much, but I've won three or four hundred dollars in an afternoon, and I very seldom lose more than twenty or thirty dollars. And I have a good time.'

'It is a good time,' Cogan said. 'It doesn't pay as good as writing the stuff down, but it's fun. I go, it's because there's other guys that're going. It's a nice thing to do, get some fresh air and see some people and maybe you even win. You lose? So what.

'Squirrel,' Cogan said, 'Squirrel don't do that. He never goes down the track, he never goes to any of the games or anything, he just bets on things. And he doesn't bet because he heard about something and he's interested in that and he thinks he's got something. He bets because he's gotta be down on something all the time, it's like he's not gonna be able to live if he's not. He thinks he's gonna win, when he bets, he's always gonna win.'

'Some people do win,' the driver said.

'I know people that win,' Cogan said. 'Some of them, get a little something in the horse and they win. Some other guys get something into all the other horses, and they win. And some guys, spent their whole lives doping horses, one or two of them, maybe there's three, I dunno, they win. Except when the other guys're getting to the animals and winning. Then they lose. And they take it in stride. Write it off. Not Squirrel. He loses today, he spent the whole morning onna phone, he's gonna be back onna phone tomorrow, and he's gonna lose again. So pretty soon he's got to go out and get some dough some place, and then something like this happens. You know Mitch?'

'Offhand,' the driver said, 'no. Never heard of a Mitch.'

'Mitch's all right,' Cogan said. 'He's a guy I know. Now, you take Mitch, he's a real gentleman. I've seen Mitch drop a grand on one race. And Mitch, he's about, oh, I dunno, he's in his fifties. Him and Dillon used to hang around together a lot. When I met Mitch, I was with Dillon. And Mitch, he does all right, but he hasn't got any more dough'n the next guy. He's from New York. So, then he goes and he bets another thousand on the next race. And I've seen him, he'll lose that and he'll maybe even double up on the next one and lose that one, too. Mitch'll drop a lot of dough. But it's something he likes to do. And the day's over, you wanna go out, you couldn't find yourself a nicer guy'n Mitch to go out with. And he runs out of dough, okay, that's it, he goes home. Nobody's got to worry about Mitch. And you won't see him playing again until next year.

'I was down to Florida there, last winter? Going again this year. Hialeah. Mitch's in town, he's staying over to that place that the two guys had that just got hooked with Lansky there. I see Mitch at the track. I ask him, what's good. And he's got a few things, he tells me: "You know me, now, Jackie. Wasn't for me, some guy'd have to invent losers, the tracks'd go out of business." He knows everybody, the jocks, the hot-walkers, everybody. They all tell him. "They all talk to me," he says, "and I listen to them, and I always take their advice and I always go home losers. I'm a lousy horse-player, is all. You can have what I got if you want it. I ever get cancer, call me up and I'll give you some of that, too, and you're such a jerk you'll probably take it." I take what he's got. We lose. We go out that night, is he pissed? Not Mitch. He's just a great guy, is all. "I been doing this a long time," he tells me. "It's not like when I went out, I didn't know what's gonna happen to me."'

'The Squirrel,' Cogan said, 'he can't do that. He loses and everything he loses, he can't afford to lose, and he gets all edgy. He gets nervous. He starts walking around. He's gonna do that, he's gonna do the other thing You know what he did? When he was inna can, he had his wife, she was making his bets for him. I heard that. And the exhibition games, the Broons? Orr's got the bad knee, they let Cheevers right out the door, nobody even tried to stop him, everybody's coasting anyway, nobody cares about those games, they're all out of shape and everything, he was betting them. He's got a good business. I asked Dillon, Dillon thinks the guy's good for at least twenty, thirty a year on that business, there's always gonna be kids coming along that want to drive. And it's not enough for him. He's an asshole.'

'Can't live on thirty thousand,' the driver said.

'My friend,' Cogan said, 'Squirrel couldn't live on ten *million*. If he got it, he'd lose it.'

'Well,' the driver said, 'it's too bad he had to lose at the card game.'

'He didn't,' Cogan said. 'He won there. He was only there twice. He had any sense, he should've kept going back there. He was the only guy in the place that could come close to knowing any-thing The guys he was playing against're bigger shits'n he is. He actually won, the two times he was there, about a thousand, eight hundred or so both times. Which of course for the Squirrel's not even carfare.

'A guy I know,' Cogan said, 'told me, Johnny Amato dropped eight thousand last week alone. Basketball. Kept missing the spread. "I love the guy," he tells me. "He thinks when you lose, it's not because you bet stupid, you probably shouldn't've got down at all. He thinks it's luck. His is just bad. That guy, he couldn't lay off of the sun coming up tomorrow, somebody was to give him a line on it, not happening." That time he was in the can, you know he just got out the can, practically?'

'What'd he do?' the driver said.

'Robbed a bank,' Cogan said. 'It was the same thing. He robbed the same bank twice. Actually got away with it once. And then he did it again. He was too far inna shit for the first time to get him out. Hadda go back and do it again, get some more dough to piss away. Got himself this bunch of ham-and-eggers and he sends them down where he does his business and he goes away. He goes down the Bahamas. They got his cars and the guns and everything, and they do it, only, of course, they're as dumb as he is, they miss about sixty and get out with no more'n thirty and he comes home. He got about five, he had so many guys in it with him, they cut it up, and anyway he got in worse shit while he was gone than he was in when he left because he dropped close to seven while he was away. Casinos're not enough for him, he was also calling home and making stupid bets on games any dumb kid'd know enough to give a leaving-alone.

'So he sets it up again,' Cogan said, 'and those dummies go back in, the people in the bank're starting to think they're gonna be regular customers or something So they're about three minutes out of the box, you ever hear of the Doctor? Eddie Mattie?'

'Yes,' the driver said, 'as a matter of fact, I have.'

'Okay,' Cogan said, 'Mattie's one of them. Now there's only one thing wrong with Mattie, which a guy might expect, he's got to have Squirrel think up things for him to do, and that's that he's fuckin'-A-number-one stupid. So he robbed a bank, right? And he's in a school zone or something, is he being very careful and everything? Not him. He's doing close to ninety and they got this lady cop there that's kind of against that, and she waves him down. *And the dumb shit stopped.* She hasn't got no cruiser, she hasn't got no gun, he's got this car if they find it the only thing they're gonna find out's that it got clouted in Plymouth about three days or so before, and he stopped. "License, registration?" He's practically gargling. So naturally the crossing guard gets herself a run in her stocking or something and about eight real cops and they take him in and there's the gun and the dough in the trunk, and he decides, he's gonna save himself. And he blabs and he blabs and he blabs. And the Squirrel's onna plane, coming home, funny thing, they had the FBI here, waiting for him, he gets off, got a nice warrant and some handcuffs. So the Squirrel and them did eight or ten. I think they should've done more, myself.'

'What'd the Doctor do?' the driver said.

'Three to five,' Cogan said. 'He was as pissed off as they were. Thought he was gonna get the street, for tipping them in.'

'Good deal for the Doctor,' the driver said. 'He must've gotten out some time ago, then.'

'Three or four years ago, I guess,' Cogan said.

'He wasn't in on this,' the driver said.

'No,' Cogan said.

'You're sure of that,' the driver said.

'I'm pretty sure, yeah,' Cogan said.

'Because he asked me to ask you about that,' the driver said.

'You can tell him, I'm very sure,' Cogan said.

'Because he never okayed anything on the Doctor,' the driver said.

'Is that so?' Cogan said.

'That's so,' the driver said. 'Told me that himself, when he asked me to ask you.'

'Of course some times,' Cogan said, 'a guy'll get a guy, and the guy'll think, the man wants it. The guy hasn't got no way of checking, you know. You just assume that.'

'I understand,' the driver said. 'This was merely something I wanted to suggest, that he wanted me to suggest. Mattie having worked with people and all. Just a question.'

'Of course everybody's got his own way of doing business,' Cogan said.

108

'Of course,' the driver said.

'Now, aside from the Squirrel,' Cogan said, 'we got the two kids. One of them's a guy that Squirrel had on the bank robberies. That one I'm sure of. The other one, I'm picking up some stuff on him, I think, but I'm not sure yet. The guy I'm talking to, he swears it's this particular kid, but I don't know.'

'What's the problem?' the driver said.

'The guy's the problem,' Cogan said. 'The guy I'm talking to. Dillon give me a couple names and I saw them and they're all-right guys but they don't know shit from Shinola about this thing. This guy I got on my own. But I don't know about him. He's close to sixty, at least, and I bet he didn't put in more'n twenty years all told on the street. Every time he did something he got nailed. So he's not very bright to begin with and now he's crazy, and I don't know about the guy, is all. I do know he's queer. He's had everything up his ass. If they're still making Packards he'd have a Packard up his ass. He's soft. You never know whether he's telling you something that happened or he's telling you something he probably dreamed was happening while nine guys're taking turns with him. I don't blame him. He's as soft as a sneaker fulla shit and he can't help it. But you got to think about what he tells you.'

'What's he tell you?' the driver said.

'There's this other kid,' Cogan said, 'this kid he knows, he knows him from the can. He probably used to blow him. He says the kid's a filthy rotten bastard, but the poor guy's scared of shadows and he'd blow dead cats if a tough kid said to, and he wants this guy, get some stuff for him. It's, he says he can get stuff like that, that you mix with the shit you're selling, and the kid asked him. Only the guy says the kid, he wanted the stuff, it's some kind of stuff dentists use, right? Makes your mouth cold.'

'Novocaine,' the driver said.

'That's what I keep thinking it is,' Cogan said. 'It's not. He told me what it is, but I can't remember. Anyway, it don't matter, it's like that, and the kid said he's gonna need about two pounds of the stuff. Now he wants four. So the guy tells me. Which means, if the guy's got it right, the kid's coming in with twice as much junk as he was gonna.'

'And that means he's got twice as much money to buy dope with,' the driver said.

'Right,' Cogan said. 'And, well, that's really all it means. I got no way of knowing, where the kid gets the dough. I'm trying to find that out. I'm also trying, find the kid. I haven't even got his whole name. This guy, ah, you can't depend on him. Either way. You can't depend on him to give you the straight shit and you can't depend on him to blow smoke up your ass. It's just a fuckin' *thing*, is all, and I dunno what I'm gonna end up doing about it.

'Now this other kid,' Cogan said, 'him I know. He was on the jobs that the Squirrel and him went in for, and he got out about the same time, and I heard it and I sent down to China and, what about this kid, could it be him? And China said: "Certainly could be." So, him I'm sure of. All we got to do now, we got to think about that other kid. He bothers me.'

'Should we move now?' the driver said. 'Or, do you want to wait.'

'I talked to Dillon about that,' Cogan said. 'Him and me, we both think: now. Games're closed, right?'

'Grant's Tomb,' the driver said.

'People're losing money,' Cogan said.

'A fair inference,' the driver said.

'They don't like losing money,' Cogan said.

'Except for Testa,' the driver said. 'He's still open.'

'So what we oughta do,' Cogan said, 'and me and Dillon both think this, you think about it and it's the only thing to do. We oughta hit Trattman now and get things started so people can get back to doing what they're supposed to be doing.'

'Trattman?' the driver said. 'What brings Trattman into this? You told me yourself, it's this Amato fellow and his friends.'

'It is,' Cogan said. 'Trattman didn't have anything to do with it. This stuff I'm getting, plus I had Trattman talked to, you're right. I had him asked and I'm sure.'

'You ought to be,' the driver said. 'Your boys went a little bit overboard there. They damn near killed the man.'

'When I talked to Steve,' Cogan said, 'I didn't know that. When I talked to you. All he told me was they worked him over and he said he didn't know anything. That's all I knew.'

'I had one hell of a time understanding him,' the driver said. 'The first time he called, I was out. My secretary talked to him. She didn't get more'n a third of what he said. I had to call him back and *I* had trouble understanding him. Hell, I had trouble, calling him back. The numbers he left, she couldn't understand what he was saying. I finally figured it out. It had to be Trattman. Cangelisi called me, all upset, and said Trattman called him and he gave me to Trattman, gave him my number. "Thanks a lot," I said. "Look," he said, "*I* didn't sic those monkeys on him. If you didn't, you know who did. You take care of him." Then when I finally reached him, I understood why the kid had trouble. He's got a broken jaw.'

'I heard that,' Cogan said.

'He's also got broken ribs and a broken nose and he got three or four teeth broken and there's something wrong with his septum,' the driver said. 'And he told me, there was some question about his spleen. He was in the hospital when I talked to him.'

'I heard some of that,' Cogan said. 'He's out now, I understand.'

'Must be his spleen's all right then,' the driver said. 'He's not happy, though.'

'Sorry to hear that,' Cogan said. 'We aim to please.'

'He'll be sorry to hear it too,' the driver said. 'When I tell him. I have to tell him.'

'Tell him anything you want,' Cogan said. 'You're his lawyer and all.'

'Trattman blames him,' the driver said. 'I didn't tell Trattman anything, of course, but you and I both know, you weren't authorized to go that far.'

'You know how guys are,' Cogan said. 'They go out to do something and they get all excited and everything. When I found out, I called Steve. He said Barry, Barry, look, Barry's an iron-worker, all right? He's a very tough guy. All of them guys carry, for Christ sake. They're always falling off something or getting into fights and stuff. He's a tough guy. That's why I use him. And Steve said, well, apparently they're about halfway along and things're going all right, and then Barry decided, Barry's very nutty about his wife. You can't talk to the guy about her. I dunno what she is, she's an angel or something. At least he says so. So, things're going along, Steve said, and Barry decides Trattman fucked his wife. She was staying some place with her mother, Barry's up in Maine on some kind of a beef, and I dunno how the hell it got started, Steve don't know either. But Barry gets this idea in his head, Trattman fucked his wife, and that's when the guy got his jaw broken and the ribs. Barry kicked him. "I oughta bitch too," Steve said to me, "I was standing too close to him and the cocksucker threw his cookies on my pants." I told him, go fuck himself.'

'Is that what I'm supposed to tell him?' the driver said. 'I was very specific when I talked to you. He told me to be. Shove him around if you want, but don't hurt him too badly. I told you he didn't want him hurt.'

'Ah, come on,' Cogan said, 'of course you did.'

'All right,' the driver said.

'You guys always do that,' Cogan said. 'I know that. You guys, you don't know how to break an egg. You want things done all right, you know what you want and the guys to go get it, and you take what you get because that's what you wanted, but you always go out after and you say, you didn't want nobody, do that. Quit shittin' me, all right? They know, they know who Steve is. They know what him and Barry do. Shit, I mean, they're guys that've always been around. When Jimmy the Fox, there, he started to get all jumpy, I had three hundred locations and there wasn't nothing left for nice ghinny boys like him, there, he started making a lot of noise and I heard about it, I turned over forty joints to Steve just like that. They all know who Steve is. They know what he does. He don't know anything. He's just a good guy to have around, and all the guys've used him.'

'The thing of it is,' the driver said, 'he didn't okay it.'

'He okayed it,' Cogan said. 'I told you who I was gonna use. He knows it just as good as I do, Steve's gonna go out and do what he thinks you want him to do. You tell him what you want, he's gonna listen, he's gonna go out and do what he thinks you want. Don't matter what you say. And, he okayed it, he had you call Dillon and he had you see me. Now cut the shit. It's not gonna make any difference anyway. We gotta hit Trattman and the man knows it.'

'I don't understand that,' the driver said. 'I thought you believed him.'

'My friend,' Cogan said, 'I do. It don't make a bit of difference. Once before, Trattman did something, right? And he was lying. He was blowing smoke up the man's ass.'

'Correct,' the driver said.

'This time,' Cogan said, 'this time Trattman didn't blow no smoke.'

'And he got beaten up,' the driver said, 'very badly beaten up.'

'But we're *sure,* this time,' Cogan said. 'This time, last time we thought we were sure and we weren't. This time we are.'

'Correct,' the driver said.

'Now,' Cogan said, 'the guys that go to the games, they're not sure. Well, they *are* sure. They're sure Trattman's got a license, because he can do it and nobody does anything about it. So that's the same thing. So what do you think they're gonna do? You think they're gonna go the games?

'And never even mind them,' Cogan said, 'what about the guys on the street? Whaddaya think they think, huh?'

'I've got no idea,' the driver said.

'They think,' Cogan said, 'they think: Trattman. He did it before and he did it again. And he lied about it before and nobody did nothing, and now he did it again and all he got was beat up.'

'He could've died,' the driver said.

'Because he stuck out,' Cogan said. 'This's his second time, the way they see it, the second time he did it. The first time you do it and if nobody catches up to you, great. The second time you can do it and somebody whales the shit out of you.'

'If that's what they think,' the driver said.

'Counselor,' Cogan said, 'take my word for it: that's what they think.'

'Ahhh,' the driver said. 'But still, he really didn't do anything.'

'It's his responsibility,' Cogan said. 'He did it before and he lied before and he fooled everybody, and, I said it to Dillon, I said: "They should've whacked him out before." And Dillon agreed with me. Now it happened again. It's his responsibility for what guys think. On the street it's Trattman, nothing but Trattman. Gets fifty, fifty-two thousand, whatever it was, he got about the same, he hadda split something, okay, but he got about the same the last time. And now they break his jaw. He's hurt and he's out what the kids cost him and he's clipped guys that trusted him about eighty thousand, and he's still walking around and everybody knows he did it.'

'He didn't do it,' the driver said. 'Not this time, anyway.'

'That's not what everybody knows,' Cogan said. 'There's lots of guys that'd drink milkshakes for a year, *if they got caught*, for that kind of dough, they had their jaws wired shut. Shit, we're gonna have kids waiting in line, knock them fuckin' games over, they open up again. You got any idea how many wild-ass junkies there are around? If he gets away with this, well, we might as well just forget it, once and for all, and just quit.'

'I still don't know,' the driver said. 'I see what you mean, the public angle, and I don't take issue with what you say about the other people. But I'm not sure how he's going to feel about this, with a man who didn't do what everybody thinks he did, when I suggest that.'

'Tell him,' Cogan said, 'ask him, where the guys come from, in the games. Not from the street. They don't care, Trattman got beat up. They're not gonna come in, is all. Trattman did it before, Trattman did it again. Trattman's through, and he can't do nothing else. Except get laid. He's good at getting laid. Otherwise he can't do nothing for us. We lose nothing there.

'Tell him also,' Cogan said, 'the guys onna street. They think the same thing, and they're gonna take what they think and nobody else's games're gonna be safe. He's hurt. Big deal. You hit a game and it's big money and the *worst* they do to you, they beat you up. The kids'll start their own union. We're gonna have nothing but guys running around for a while, knocking down doors worse'n cops, and then after a while there's not gonna be no games, no games at all. "Goin' to a game? Right. Save yourself some time. Go inna room, put your hands up, throw the cash onna bed, you get home early and the wife's glad and you didn't take no chances, getting yourself shot." Guys're not gonna go for it, and there's no two ways about it.'

'Counselor,' Cogan said, 'go talk to the man. Trattman's gotta be hit, and you put it up to the man, he'll agree with me right off. Give it a try. You don't do it? Forget about the money. He made a mistake.'

'A long time ago,' the driver said. 'He made a mistake a long time ago.'

'He made two mistakes,' Cogan said. 'The second mistake was making the first mistake, like it always is. That's all you get, two mistakes. Tell the man.'

'If he agrees with you,' the driver said, 'assuming that. You can hit Trattman?'

'Yeah,' Cogan said.

'How about this Amato fellow?' the driver said. 'He seems like the leading candidate to me.'

'He's right up there,' Cogan said. 'Not yet. Wait'll we do Trattman. It'll make him easier, we do that. But sooner or later, yeah.'

'Can you handle?' the driver said.

'Right now,' Cogan said, 'probably not. Not the way things are right now.'

'Who?' the driver said. 'He knows people, of course, but he always wants to know who was suggested by the fellow I talk to.'

'I got a couple things in mind,' Cogan said. 'That one, I got to think about that one, and I got to make sure. Maybe, maybe we're gonna need Mitch.'

'He does this kind of thing?' the driver said.

'Let's think about Trattman for now,' Cogan said. 'Later on, we can start to think about what guys do. But yeah, Mitch's been at it a long time. One of the best.'

9

'It was fuckin' beautiful,' Russell said. He sat on the trunk of the GTO and Frankie leaned against a parking meter. The car was parked in front of the Chicken In the Box on Cambridge Street in Boston.

'We leave inna middle of the night, for Christ sake,' Russell said. 'I said to him: "For Christ sake, Kenny, we're gonna have to drive inna daytime sooner or later, there's no way we're stoppin' anywhere with what we're gonna have in there. So why the fuck're we leaving when we oughta be in bed?"'

'"Well," he tells me, "see, we gotta do it this way. I wanna get the hell at least onna Jersey Pike before it gets light. Too many fuckin' cops around here, heard about fuckin' dogs missing. See a couple guys, carful of dogs, they're maybe gonna get around to stopping us, see what we got to say." But cops other places, they didn't hear nothing about dogs, nobody told them anything. "And besides," he says, "I did this before. First part of the trip's really something. So, we start inna dark." '

'Then he shows up,' Russell said. 'See, I couldn't sleep. He told me: "Get yourself six, seven hours in the afternoon, you can. We got about sixteen hundred miles in front of us. Last time, took me almost three days. So it'd really help, you get some sleep, all them dogs inna car and everything." '

'Okay,' Russell said, 'I try it. I get up. I eat. I sit around. I let my fuckin' dogs *out*. I let my fuckin' dogs *in*. I feed my fuckin' dogs. That's another thing he tells me. "When've you been feeding them dogs? At night, probably." I tell him, yeah, just before I go out, the horsemeat and the fuckin' meal. Keeps them nice and quiet. "Tomorrow," he says, "feed them, lunch instead. Dogs don't know the difference. I want them dogs have a good shit for themselves, before we get them inna car. Also, now, I want you to give them something, all right?" '

'I thought he means the phenobarb,' Russell said. 'Christ, I got myself so much phenobarb I could nod off half the town without doing nothing else. No. Because, see, you dope them just before you load them up, inna car, they all start off with a nice nap. He's got mineral oil. Four fuckin' gallons of mineral oil.

' "Dump this in their fuckin' food," he says. "Give 'em fuckin' all of it. Got any tomato soup? Get about twenny cans tomato soup, mix that up and heat it, right? Just like you're gonna eat it yourself." I tell him, I can't eat it, it hasn't got rice in it. "Always tomato rice inna slammer, Kenny," I say. "I gotta put rice in it?" He doesn't know anything. The guy's got absolutely no sense of humor and he never did time. He don't know anything.'

'He should've,' Frankie said.

'There's very few guys,' Russell said, 'shouldn't've. "Look," he says, "heat it up and dump the oil in. Then pour it in their food and they'll woof it down like champs. Otherwise, they won't. Then, I guarantee it, you make sure them fuckin' dogs can get out, fast, because that stuff's gonna come out of them like they're *waxed*."'

'Them dogs,' Russell said, 'all I could think of was when guys got dysentery the first time, you know? And they didn't, they never had nothing like you get there, before that, and they didn't know what was gonna happen to them. So them dogs, I put that food down, they practically trample each other, get at it, and I let them out and pretty soon they're all wrinkled up, their faces're all wrinkled and they're squatting and squatting. Christ, you could smell that fuckin' backyard in goddamned Springfield, steam's coming out of the grass like it's on fire or something. My mother comes home, she's about a block away and she starts in on me. "Where're you getting them dogs from? They'll have the Board of Health down." I said: "Yeah, Ma. You know what you did? You hurt my feelings. You shouldn't've come down here, you should've stayed where you are." My only son, he's in jail, she's got to come down here so she can be around and visit me. Know how many times she visits me? Three times. Three times in almost three years. Brought me a fuckin' cake, once. They wouldn't let her bring it in. "Shouldn't've put the file in it, Ma," I said, "I meant to tell you, Ma, they got the metal detector, there. They can spot the file." She tells me: "There was nothing in that cake." Fine mother she is, I tell her. Shit. I said: "Ma, you hurt my feelings. Just for that, I'm gonna take my dogs out of here. I'm gonna take 'em out tonight. But just for that, I'm not cleaning up. I was you, taking the garbage out, I think I'd wanna be careful where I was stepping." She looks at me. "Figures," she says, "fits right in with everything else I got from you. Do me a favor, willya? Don't come back." I told her: "I take after my old man. I won't." '

'Now the next thing I got to do,' Russell said, 'I got to get that phenobarb into them dogs. "This's kind of tricky," he tells me. "You got to take the water away from them by five o'clock, because them dogs, after the oil goes through them they'll drink it all, and then we'll fuckin' *drown* in dogpiss. The trouble is, the last time I did this we give them the phenobarb about five, before we take the water away from them, and we really gave them a lot, because the time before that we didn't give them enough and they got inna car and they all hadda nice nap and then it's a fuckin' madhouse. So the last time we give them too much and they're all woozy, we get them to the guy, and we didn't get nothing for them, the dogs're sick and all the rest of it. I don't want no more of that shit. I don't want them dogs raising hell all the way down and I don't want them bumping into things, we get down there, either. Give the little ones, half a grain. A grain if they're lively. The big ones a couple grains, and if they're, if there's any of them that're still jumping round, hit 'em again. With the water. Then take the water back. Take some bread and make it in little balls and stick another half a grain in that and give them it around eleven or so, and that oughta do it." '

'I said to him,' Russell said, 'I said: "Kenny, I thought I was supposed to sleep all day. How'm I gonna sleep, I'm doing all them things?" And he tells me. "Take a little dog dope." So I ask him, he's gettin' dough offa these dogs, how come I got to do all the work? "Well," he says, "I got to do something." '

'He's worse'n fuckin' Squirrel for making out off guys,' Russell said. 'He shows up, right around midnight, he's got three more dogs. I'm busting my ass all day, getting dogs ready, Kenny's out gettin' more dogs. I said: "For Christ sake, Kenny, that's" – we already sold some of the dogs to this guy down the North End? Poodles. We had three poodles and he give us a buck and a half apiece on them. Which isn't bad – "that's sixteen dogs we got, mine and yours." He's got this Caddy limo. Took the back seat out and he had a lot of old blankets all the way back in there, in the trunk. "Can't put sixteen dogs in there. They'll kill each other."'

'These dogs, he tells me, "These're little ones." He's got a couple spaniels and a wire-haired. "Fit right in, no sweat." So, we load them up. My dogs're all dopey. He takes the front legs, I take back legs. My mother's looking out of the window. Finally get all them dogs in. Stack them right up. I'm getting in the car, she opens the window. "That all of them?" Yeah. "Good. Remember what I said." Right, and now I understand the old man a lot better, too. She shuts the window, bang.'

'You're still better off'n I was,' Frankie said. 'My mother, she used to come every week. Every single fuckin' week, I'd, I used to sit on Sunday, and the first thing I hadda do was, I hadda go to Mass. Fuckin' guy, every single fuckin' week he talks about Dismas. Oh for Christ sake. Well, no. Some weeks he talks about beating off. Funny, didn't have nothing to say about blow jobs and like that. And then, the good meal, you know? The one that was just as shitty as the rest of them, except it was supposed to be good. Seen a turnip? I see another turnip, I throw the fuckin' thing at somebody. And then my poor old gray-haired mother, her and her fuckin' coat that's all beat to shit, comes in looking like somebody that just got hit on the head. And I got to sit through that. "I pray for you, Frankie" "I made a novena for you, Frankie." "I hope you get parole, Frankie." "I know in my heart you're a good boy, Frankie" "Frankie, you've got to change your ways." And she's gonna stay, boy, she's not comin' all the way up there, she's gonna leave in five minutes. No, sir. One week she's sick. Sandy comes for a change. "Anything I can do for you, Frankie?" You bet your ass there is. Chain Ma the bed, for Christ sake. "She don't mean anything," Sandy says. "She feels guilty. She told me, she dunno what she didn't do." I told her: "She didn't tell me about assholes like the Doctor, that's what it is," ' Frankie said. ' "Tell her, the next kid, teach him to plan a job right, he doesn't get some fatmouth bastard in there, fuck things up." She looks at me. "You want me to tell her, you don't want her coming no more?" Of course I do. So she does, and the next week Ma comes up, you should've seen her. Looked like somebody took her out and kicked the shit out of her. "*Frankie*," she says, "Sandy said, you don't want your mother coming up here no more." And then she starts crying, and there's guys looking at me, and half of them're bulls and they're all gonna tell the parole, "He's mean to his mother, she comes up to see him and he don't appreciate it." Oh, Jesus, it was awful. So, what could I do? I told her, come back, Ma, I was just talking. And she did. Novenas, the stations, the rosary, she's going down to Mission Church there and everything for me. Christ. "I ain't crippled, Ma," I tell her. "In your soul you are," she says. Jesus. I'm lucky I didn't get at her through the screen.'

'They don't know,' Russell said. 'None of them know. They just think, you're in there, you can't get out. That's all they know. They don't know.'

'I wished they did,' Frankie said. 'Putting up with them's something awful. I wished I knew what it was, a guy goes in and they think it isn't bad enough, they got to make it worse. I go in again, boy, I'm making sure nobody knows. I dunno if I can do time again, but I sure can't take the visiting. Shit.'

'I'm not going in again,' Russell said. 'That's what I'm not gonna do.'

'You decided, huh?' Frankie said.

'I'm doing everything I can,' Russell said.

'And that's what's gonna put you in again,' Frankie said.

'Nah,' Russell said.

'Sure,' Frankie said, 'you're going back for stealing dogs.'

'Not so far,' Russell said, 'and never again, either. You know something? The next dog I see, I'm gonna do a wheelie on him, is what I'm gonna do. Dogs, dogs're stupid. You beat the living shit out of a dog, hit him with the pills and he goes to sleep, he wakes up the next day and he's staggering around and all, but he's hungry. All you got to do with a dog, you can do anything you want to a dog, then just wait till he gets hungry and feed him and he thinks you're fuckin' God or something. Except that black fucker.'

'Shepherd grab you?' Frankie said.

'That dog,' Russell said, 'he's the only dog I ever saw, remembers. First time he wakes up, sees me, rrrr, way down in his throat. So, I give him another day. Gets hungry enough, he'll come around. I starved that fucker *four days*. His bones showed, for Christ sake. Know what I get when I go out? Rrrrr. I thought I was gonna have to give him some more of the stick. But he don't come after me, see? Which proves it, that black bastard isn't dumb. He remembers that stick. He's not gonna tackle me. He's just gonna make my life as hard's he possibly can. So, I hadda feed him. I can't sell hairy bones, for Christ sake.

'Now,' Russell said, 'now he's got me, and he knows it. I try and get him out, he holds back. I practically got to throw him out of the garage. Then he won't, I can't get him in. And he growls at me

124

all the time, still. That bastard, all the way to Florida, we're in this fuckin' rainstorm in Maryland, they had a barge hit the bridge and we either hadda go around or we use the tunnel. Which everybody else is using. So Kenny say, "We're going around." I thought I seen rain when I was with my Uncle. Christ. And them dogs're all pissing and farting and shitting and everything in there and we can't leave the windows down, we don't wanna suffocate, and we also don't want to drown. It was awful. I thought dogs was an easy way to make money. It's not dangerous. I was right about that. I was half right. You know what I get for that black fucker, I thought I was probably gonna get twenty million dollars or something? Seventy-five bucks I got for that dog, and I was lucky to get that. The guy we're selling them to, he just buys them, right? He just, he only takes care of them. One of those guys with no meat on him. He doesn't talk. We're there, he's got this kind of beaten-to-shit old farm down outside Cocoa Beach. We're there about half an hour, we're finally breathing again, we been on the road about ten years with them dogs, all of a sudden I notice, his wife does all the talking. "This one here looks like he's been run over," she says. She never stops talking and he never starts. "He sick or something? We don't want no sick dogs here, Mister. I can't let you have more'n twenty dollars for this one." '

'So I say to her,' Russell said, 'she said she's gonna give me fifty bucks for the black one. "Look, he's got papers, he's a valuable dog. He's the real thing. He's a great dog. Fifty's not enough." '

' "He hasn't got no papers today, Mister," she says to me,' Russell said. ' "He's just another dog now that I got to think about selling to somebody and that means I got to keep him and feed him and look after him the whole time I'm trying to sell him to somebody, and that's going to be a long time. I don't want this dog. I don't want him at all. You want to take him back with you? Because that's exactly what you can do, if you don't like the price. I'll have trouble, selling that dog to somebody. He looks vicious to me and he'll look vicious to somebody else.'

'The guy still doesn't say anything,' Russell said. 'Now, she's got me, of course. I'm not taking that dog no place with me ever again. What I want to say to that dog is "Good-bye," and I hope I never see him again. All the way to Florida that bastard's watching the back of my neck, he's gonna eat me if he gets half a chance. She's right. He is vicious. But, he's not being vicious then. The guy's got him sitting down and the dog's giving him his paw and the guy's rubbing his ears and that dog is fuckin' grinning at him. He thinks he's home again with the stupid bastard that bought him to protect the medals. Then the dog, the guy stands up and the dog stands up too, puts his feet on the guy's shoulders and starts lapping his face. "Look, Lady," I say, "that's a vicious dog? You think somebody's gonna think that's a vicious dog? Let 'em see him like that."'

'"Mister," she says, "that's the way he is. That's the way they all are with him. Every dog that comes in here's like that. That's why he keeps the dogs and I do the business. Fifty."'

'The guy wakes up or something,' Russell said. 'He looks at us. The shepherd's frenching him, for Christ sake. Guy finally gets the dog's tongue out of his mouth. "Give him seventy-five, Imelda," he says.'

'"Seventy-five," she says,' Russell said. '"Now," she says, takes her about three hours to say anything, "am I setting the prices here, or are you gonna argue with me every time he decides he likes another dog? Because if you are, you can leave right now and take the rest of those animals with you." The only thing I wish,'

Russell said, 'I wish that woman could've met my mother. They'd get along fuckin' great.'

'You got out of there all right, though,' Frankie said.

'Yeah,' Russell said. 'Went over to Orlando with Kenny, burn the fuckin' car. Kenny fuckin' near killed himself. Went in this orange grove, right? Pulled it offa the road, there's this little dirt road, there. So, Kenny was driving. He gets out, sticks a rag down the gas tank, he hangs it down and soaks it and then he pulls it out and hangs it down onna fender and lights it off. Fuckin' car just blew up. And, he left it in gear, you know? Knocked him right on his ass, it was in reverse. He's a hot shit. Gets up. "Okay," he says, "that's the second job like that I fucked up. I got to do that again, I'm gonna find somebody, knows what he's doing." Kenny, he didn't have no eyebrows, for Christ sake, hasn't got much hair left, either.'

'What was it,' Frankie said, 'hot?'

'Nah,' Russell said, 'it was Kenny's car. But what the fuck's a car good for, you had all them dogs in it over two days? Nothin'. It's like riding in a shithouse. So, Kenny had it in his sister's name, she called the cops the day we're supposed to get there, says it got stolen. Then, we got out of there Wednesday. You should've seen those assholes when they search you at the airport, they see me and Kenny. I thought their eyes was gonna come right out of their heads. Four times we got to go through the metal detector. Then there was this guy, I guess he was the newest guy there or something, he had to pat us down. I think they give him the rest of the day off. "You're gonna let us on the plane, finally," Kenny said, "aren't you?" They look at him. "Mister," one of them says, "if you haven't got no weapons on you, you can ride. You prob- ably oughta ride in the baggage, but never mind that." Nobody'd sit next to us. We hadda ride way in the back and there was this one stewardess, every time she hadda come near us, she'd look at us like she never saw anything like us before in her life. "You guys going all the way to Boston?" she says. "You wouldn't consider, getting off in Washington or some place?" Kenny fell for it. "This thing gonna land in Washington?" he says. "I never been to Washington." See, we didn't stop or anything. "No," she says, "but if you'll get off there, I'll use my influence with the captain and I'm sure he'll agree to it." The guy on the bus from New York,' Russell said, 'I come up from there onna bus? I'm not gonna get searched with the weight on me. I thought he was gonna make me ride outside. I fuckin' crashed when I got here, boy. I never been so tired in my life.'

'You look all beat to shit,' Frankie said.

'Yeah,' Russell said, 'and the hell of it is, I been up for about a week, you know? And I shouldn't've even slept last night, only I hadda or I would've just fallen down. I got to keep moving till I finish this thing off. I thought I was gonna see the guy with the other stuff this morning, but I couldn't raise him.'

'You haven't dumped the stuff?' Frankie said.

'Dump it,' Russell said, 'Christ, no. I didn't hit it yet. I can't, I probably won't be able to move it till tonight, now, by the time I see him and everything. I know where it is. I can get it, and I haven't got it on me.'

'Down the bus station,' Frankie said.

'Never mind,' Russell said. 'I know where it is.'

'You're just an asshole,' Frankie said. 'You know that, you asshole? The kind of chances you're taking, they're gonna forget about putting you away for the stuff when they catch you. They're gonna put you away for being nuts.'

'Talk to me about that when I get the dough,' Russell said.

'Russ,' Frankie said, 'this whole town's dry, and it's been dry for three or four weeks. There's more guys running into drugstores now with guns'n you ever saw. They got Goldfinger and that was the end of that. They tossed three guys with shipments this week, for Christ sake. The minute the word gets out, somebody's in with something, everybody goes right out of their minds. There's more heat in this town on that'n there is in the FBI, for Christ sake. Unload, Russ. Let somebody else do a hundred years or so, they catch him with it.'

'Not till I hit it,' Russell said. 'Look, I'm into this, over twelve K, right? I put it to a guy, fast, I don't hit it, what do I get? I'm gonna get, even with things the way they are, no more'n fifteen, sixteen. I take it up a step, I can hit that stuff a whole step with the stuff I'm getting, I can move it to two guys and get twenny-five.'

'It's stupid,' Frankie said. 'It's fuckin' stupid. That's a thousand dollars a year.'

'Look,' Russell said, 'I don't need nothing, make me dumb. You know that, you and Squirrel. Squirrel knows it, at least. Maybe you still think we were smart, doing that. You're just as dumb as I am. You just come around and stroke me some, I'll do any dumb fuckin' thing you can think of. The thing is, though, you and me're different. When this's over, I'm through, doing dumb things for guys. I do dumb things for me, maybe, and then, I get grabbed, okay, at least I was doing them for me. Which means, I get to keep all the fuckin' money. I don't have to give Squirrel nothing for being smart enough to see I'm stupid any more.'

'That worked out beautiful,' Frankie said.

'Sure,' Russell said, 'fuckin' cheesecake. Of course there's a contract out on us and all, but it worked beautiful. You and me, we got different ideas of beautiful, too.'

'The fuck're you talking about?' Frankie said.

'You,' Russell said, 'me, and the Squirrel. There's a contract out on us. I hang around here too long, which I'm not gonna do, I'm gonna be as dead as you guys are. I'm gonna go to Montreal. I know a guy that's got something going up there and that's where I'm gonna go. And I'll tell you something: if I didn't, I'd still go.'

'For what?' Frankie said.

'Cut the shit, Frank,' Russell said, 'for the Trattman game. The fuck's the matter with you?'

'What the fuck's the matter with *you*?' Frankie said. 'You're the one that's got something the matter with him. Where're you getting this fairy story? You flying or something?'

'Frank,' Russell said, 'I can add and subtract. There's gotta be a contract. Has to be one.'

'Nobody knows we did it,' Frankie said.

'I think they do,' Russell said.

'They went for it,' Frankie said.

'That's good,' Russell said. 'You go ahead and believe that. It'll make you feel better while the guy's catching up with you. Who's the guy that does the work? Tell him when he sees you, sorry I couldn't wait around. Tell him I went to, tell him I went back inna service, I liked it better when it was a pretty good chance I'd at least get a chance to shoot back if they missed me the first time.'

'Russell,' Frankie said, 'Trattman's practically dead. They beat him shitless. You didn't know that, did you?'

'Shit,' Russell said, 'of course I knew that. Kenny told me that.'

'Kenny,' Frankie said, 'this's Kenny Gill we're talking about, right?'

'Right,' Russell said. 'Kenny was telling me, well, he didn't give me the guy's name, but it hadda be Trattman. We're talking, we got all them fuckin' dogs inna car and we got all this time and it's raining and everything, I said to him. "You know, this really sucks. This is really a shitty way to make a couple dollars. I thought it was gonna be easy, and it fuckin' sucks."

'"Well," he tells me, we get to talking, "there's not very many things a guy can do." And he tells me, there's a guy, runs a card game some place, Kenny don't even know who he is.'

'Bull*shit*,' Frankie said.

'No bullshit,' Russell said, 'he didn't know the guy's name.'

'Kenny Gill works for Dillon,' Frankie said.

'So fuckin' what?' Russell said.

'Anything Kenny knows, he got from Dillon,' Frankie said. 'He's too goddamned stupid to figure out anything for himself. If Kenny knows a guy who runs a card game, Dillon knows, and there was some kind of reason he had for telling Kenny. Nobody ever tells Kenny nothing unless it's something they got to tell him because they want him to do something for them.'

'They did,' Russell said, 'that's what he said. He said there's this guy, he knows these two guys, him and his brother hadda go out and do the number onna guy that runs a card game. Hadda be Trattman. Because the guy knocked over his own game and they hadda teach him something for a change. And them guys, well, Kenny knows them, is all, and they asked him if he wanted to come along, they'd give him some of the money, but he was going with me and the dogs and he couldn't. That's all. "I give that up," he was saying. "It don't pay anything and it's dangerous. I bet them guys didn't get more'n two hundred bucks, and look at the chances they hadda take, huh?

The fuck can you do with a hundred bucks. Nothin'." That's all he said.'

'Yeah,' Frankie said, 'and what'd you say, case Dillon didn't have the whole story before?'

'I didn't say shit,' Russell said.

'You horse's cock,' Frankie said.

'I didn't say fuckin' shit,' Russell said. 'The guy told me something. I listened. He never even, I didn't, if I didn't already know something, I wouldn't even've known it was Trattman. You think I was gonna say something, the guy's telling me they just beat up a guy that they know did it before? They just beat him up? Is that all they're gonna do to him? No, I said nothing. Shit, all I could think about was not saying anything, and getting out of here before they find out I'm back.'

'You better not've,' Frankie said. 'John's gonna be mad as hell about this.'

'Oh,' Russell said, 'big fuckin' deal. I got the Squirrel mad. I'll probably have to go to bed without no fuckin' supper. Fuck him.'

10

'You think he did,' Amato said.

'John,' Frankie said, 'I *know* he did. Him and Kenny're in that car for three days. Non-fuckin'-stop. He must've spilled his fuckin' guts. I know the guy. I never would've figured him for it, but it's the only thing that could've happened. He was trying to warn me, is all. He finally seen what he did and he was trying to tell me, I'm inna shit. You and me both.'

'So's he,' Amato said.

'Not in Montreal,' Frankie said. 'In Montreal he's as clean as he can be.'

'There's guys in Montreal, too, you know,' Amato said.

'I know it,' Frankie said, 'and you know it. He apparently doesn't. It don't make no difference. It's what he thinks. He thinks we're inna shit around here, and the thing that proves it is, he thinks he is, and he thinks so from talking too much to a guy that works for Dillon. Kenny must've said something, finally, that tipped him. That's why.'

'You brought him in,' Amato said. 'I asked you all kinds of things about him, you remember. You said he was all right. Remember that?'

'I made a mistake,' Frankie said. 'How the fuck'd I know this was gonna happen? He was Mister Tight-Asshole before, there was nothing you could've done to the guy, make him say anything. I thought he'd do it and that'd be the end of it. I didn't know he was gonna go to Confession to Kenny Gill.'

'You used to hand me a good deal of shit about the Doctor,' Amato said. 'He was all my fault.'

'He was your mistake,' Frankie said. 'I did a lot of time for your mistake. Now what I want, I don't want to get dead for my mistake. I tell you what, we get this straightened out? You can give me all kinds of shit if you want. I know it. I didn't know he was motor-mouth, but I brought him in and he was. Okay, so what do we do now? I didn't know he was gonna start off and be the big operator. "I can't waste no time, I just knock over this guy's game for a hundred thou." I thought he was smart. Now I see, he wasn't, and he's gonna save his ass and then we get the shit. Fuck him.'

'You're sure about this Gill kid,' Amato said.

'I'm surer about him'n I am about fuckin' God,' Frankie said. 'Ever go the zoo, see an ape? That's Kenny. Looks like a fuckin' ape, he's all bowlegged and he's got real short legs, too. This huge body, and he walks, he walks like a fuckin' monkey. Hands practically drag onna ground when he walks. You looked at him, you'd think somebody skinned him and put a pair of pants on him and took away his fuckin' club. And, he's stupid. He knows things, he knows how to do things, because somebody told him and he listened and the guy talked real slow, too, nice and loud. Kenny can listen. Otherwise, he's stupid. His idea of talking is, he listens, and somebody asks him something, he goes uh, uh, uh. That's when he feels good. When he don't feel good, he don't say anything. You ask him something, he'll sit there and he'll stare at you, and he thinks about it. He tries to think about it. He's not very good and he's not very fast. You got an hour or so, he'll do his best. That's what he does. Then he might say something. It'll be just the same thing you said to him. He always agrees with you. Kenny knows about, probably, two things. You hit one of them, you can talk. Otherwise, no. And he breathes. He's good at breathing.'

'Ah,' Amato said, 'well, at least he shouldn't be too tough.'

'He did work for Dillon,' Frankie said.

'Wyatt Earp did things for Dillon,' Amato said. 'The way I get it, I seen him myself, don't forget, don't matter what anybody did for Dillon. Dillon's gonna die.'

'You remember Callahan?' Frankie said.

'No,' Amato said.

'Sure,' Frankie said, 'the lawyer, there. Used to work for the man some times. Car blew up.'

'Right,' Amato said.

'Kenny Gill did that,' Frankie said.

'That happened,' Amato said, 'we're inna can.'

'That's how I found out, it's Kenny,' Frankie said. 'China told me, he was up onna habe and his wife give him the word. Six sticks on the fire wall.'

'That's an awful way to do a guy,' Amato said.

'Callahan'd agree with you,' Frankie said, 'lost most of his stuff in that. Blew his ass off, for one thing. Would've gotten all of him if he had the door all the way closed, he hit the switch. China told me: "Kenny's nuts. He'd do anything Dillon told him, Dillon said: 'Kenny, cut your dick off,' Kenny'd cut his dick off, take it right out and start chopping away. There's a lot of guys around that're afraid of Dillon and they don't even know it's Kenny they're really afraid of." '

'I better have Connie start the car inna morning?' Amato said.

'That's an idea,' Frankie said, 'and if it don't go off, have her drive over and start mine for me. No, but we got to think of something. I thought, the first thing I thought of, we oughta take Russell out. That's the very first thing I thought of to do. I don't like it, I never did nothing like that, but that son of a bitch, if I'm in the hole, he's the one that got me there, and I could kill him for it, I really could.'

'That gonna be such a good idea?' Amato said.

'No,' Frankie said. 'He already did the damage anyway, and if we put him to sleep it'll just prove it to everybody, that we're the guys that did it. One way or the other, he's gonna go anyway. He's either right, and they're gonna kill us all, or else he's gonna go to Canada or he's gonna get caught with that stuff and go to the jug and he's never gonna come out again. No, right now the main thing we got to worry about is Kenny. I don't think they're gonna send Kenny around to see me. I know him and I wouldn't let him get inside a block of me, I'd take him out. So they got to get somebody else, and that's gonna take them a little time.'

'Plus which,' Amato said, 'I wonder if they'd do it, the way things're going right now. Too much noise.'

'They'd do it,' Frankie said. 'We got to start being very careful and looking around and everything.'

'No,' Amato said, 'nope, I can't figure it. It was Trattman's game got hit. It was Trattman got beat up. Trattman didn't have no other reason, get beat up, and they don't go around beating guys like that up like that for the fun of it. Nope, they're not looking for us. Nobody's even thinking about that thing any more.'

'John,' Frankie said, 'look, I hope you're right. I wanna live a long time. I just got started and I like it.'

'I'm right,' Amato said.

'You don't mind, though,' Frankie said, 'I look around a little.'

'Frankie,' Amato said, 'get as nervous as you like. We did it and we're clear. I'm going over to Brockton a couple more times and tend to business. I'll let you know when it's time to stop worrying and go to work again.'

11

In the early afternoon, Cogan drank a stein of dark in Jake Wirth's. He sat far back, on the bar side, and watched the bar door. In the dining area, beyond the brass rail, medical technicians and the interns hustling them sat in white jackets and drank steins of dark and gossiped about the New England Medical Center.

Mitch came through the bar door. He scanned the room quickly, found Cogan and started across the wooden floor and the sawdust. He wore a plain Harris Tweed sports coat and gray flannel slacks and a dark blue shirt, open at the throat. His hair was black and short. He had very light skin. At the table he offered his hand and said: 'Jack.'

They shook hands. Cogan said: 'Mitch.' They sat down. Cogan signaled one of the waiters; he raised two fingers.

'Uh uh,' Mitch said.

'Wagon?' Cogan said.

'Gettin' fat,' Mitch said. The waiter approached. 'Beefeater martini,' Mitch said. 'Onna rocks. Olive. Right?' The waiter nodded.

'You had lunch?' Cogan said.

'Onna plane,' Mitch said. 'I had lunch onna plane. Some lunch.'

'Oughta have the goulash,' Cogan said. 'Basically it's beef stew, but they put tomatoes and stuff in it. It's pretty good.'

'They still got that place down the alley, all the bums go and you can get beef stew there?' Mitch said.

'Conway and Downey's,' Cogan said, 'yeah. Isn't that great beef stew?'

'I used to think so,' Mitch said. 'Dillon took me in there one time. "Jesus," I said, "you know all the good joints, don't you?" It was one of those lousy days, snowing and everything, Christ, you couldn't get around any place, and we're having all kinds of problems with this guy and Dillon took me in there. He got all pissed off. Any time you want to piss Dillon off, make him think you think he's doing something bush. Sets him right off. That and telling him there's nothing the matter with him. I guess there is, though, huh?'

'This time there is,' Cogan said.

'Son of a bitch,' Mitch said. 'I dunno, I guess, shit, I'm fifty-one years old and I'm getting fat. I don't know, I never had no trouble with my weight. I was about thirty, thirty-five, Jesus, you know something? When I was thirty, for Christ sake, you know who was fuckin' President? Harry fuckin' Truman.'

'He's about a hundred years old now,' Cogan said.

'For all I know,' Mitch said, 'he's fuckin' dead. I dunno. I used to, I used to cut down onna potatoes then, that's all I had to do. No more problem. Work out now and then, lay off the potatoes. I could always have a glass of beer when I wanted one.'

'Maybe more'n one,' Cogan said.

'Well,' Mitch said, "once or twice, maybe. But I could do it, then. Now, now I can't do it. Now, I look at a glass of beer, I get fat. Pisses me off. It's that cortisone I was taking, you know? It bloats you. I was, I said to the doctor, I told him, this stuff's gonna get me so fat I'll die of that. And he tells me, no, soon's I stop taking it, I'll go right down again. But I didn't." '

'What're you on cortisone for?' Cogan said.

'Colitis,' Mitch said. 'I was sick last spring, the summer. I really felt shitty. I didn't take that much of it, you know? I wasn't on it for that long. Except, well, I almost got real sick. I was, I hadda see the cock doctor and he gimme penicillin, and I didn't bother to tell him, I'm onna cortisone, and I guess you're not supposed to do that, mix them two things like that. I was really sick for about a week or so. Couldn't get or do anything.'

'My wife had to take that stuff,' Cogan said, 'that cortisone. I think it was that. Maybe it was something else. She didn't gain that much weight, though.'

'She got arthritis or something?' Mitch said.

'Poison oak,' Cogan said. 'She likes to be outdoors all the time she can, she's got this real nice garden. And she was out there and she got this poison oak. So, she didn't think anything about it, probably pulled some roots or something she shouldn't've, and the next thing you know, well, she's covered with that calomine lotion all the time and she's itchy and it just wouldn't go away. So she finally went the doctor, and he tells her, it's in her bloodstream, and that's when she started taking the stuff. It got in her hair, you know? It was all over her scalp and down behind her ears and everything She gets up before me, she goes to work earlier'n I do, and it used to wake me up, she was in the bathroom, crying, it hurt so bad to comb her hair. So they said, we're never gonna beat it putting things on it, we're gonna have to have you take something. I think it was cortisone. She really went through hell there, for a while.'

'She'll probably get it again next year, too, then,' Mitch said.

'I know it,' Cogan said. 'I asked the doctor that, and he said no, that's just if it gets in your blood and you don't take nothing for it to kill it, then it comes back again if you just put stuff on it. But I wouldn't be surprised. Them guys don't always know what they're doing. See, the big problem with her, is, she's got, she's always had this real bad problem with bugs, you know? Bees and hornets and stuff. She's allergic to them.'

'Swells all up and everything?' Mitch said. 'When I was a kid I used to do that.'

'Worse'n that,' Cogan said, 'she could actually die. She's got, she never leaves the house, she hasn't got a needle with her, adrenalin, I got one in the glove box in the car, I got one in the truck. They told her, you get stung, you get stung above the neck, you got five minutes to get that shot. Twenny minutes below the neck. They told me: "Hit her the shot. Don't try to get her to the hospital. You won't have time. Her heart'll stop." '

'Jesus,' Mitch said, 'that's a tough thing.'

'She's a tough girl,' Cogan said. 'She's lived like that most of her life. "There're bees in the world," she says. "I can't stay inside all my life. What if a bee comes inside?" She told me, she got stung a couple years ago, we're having dinner, this place right on the water and I guess they're hiving underneath it or something and, she don't wear no perfume, of course, and I generally got more brains but somebody gave me some of that Brut and I had it on, and one of the bees comes out and I guess he was probably

141

looking for me. So he lands on her neck and the waiter sees it and, he's gonna be helpful, he tries to brush it away. I didn't see what he was doing, he was already doing it. Well, he missed, and the way he did it, he drove the stinger right in and she *screams.* And she goes for her bag and she starts to turn blue. Well, I had the one I carry, and I practically knock the tables over, getting around to her, and she can't get no breath, you know? So I give her the shot and she's all right. "Feels just like everybody took all the air out of the world," she says.

'And every so often,' Cogan said, 'she puts up with all of this, she knows what can happen to her, we got to go down and see her old lady, and Carol's got two sisters, all right? And they each got about a million kids and Carol's good with them. And her mother hasn't got no sense. She gets this look on her face. She don't have to *say* anything. Just sits there. And she knows what Carol's got, of course, but she looks at her and my wife's tough. "Ma," she'll say, "*Aunt* Carol'll have to be the limit, is all. You can't always do the things you'd like to do." '

'You can't never do the things you'd like to do,' Mitch said. 'Never. Every time you do, you get inna shit. Look at Dillon.'

The waiter, having served the interns and technicians twice, brought the drinks to Cogan and Mitch.

'First of the day,' Mitch said. 'Except for the ones I had on the plane, anyway.' He drank. 'Buck and a half for a stinking drink,' he said. 'They oughta be ashamed of themselves. Fuckin' bandits. No, look at Dillon. There's a guy. I never seen the guy do too much of anything. He'd take a drink, he liked a big meal now and then, I guess he used to get a broad when he needed one. I dunno, I never saw him, but I assume he did.'

'He used to go and see his wife some times,' Cogan said.

'She was a beauty,' Mitch said. He finished the drink. He signaled the waiter. 'He told me once, he caught her going through his pockets. I told him: "I'd kill a broad I caught doing that." And you know what he told me? "No," he says, "I always like to know, anybody that's around me, how far he's willing to go. Now, about her, I know." I dunno, I think Dillon's had a pretty lousy time. The only time I ever saw him doing anything, have any fun, was that time he was down in Florida, there. Too bad for the guy. Did the same thing all his life, I dunno. I wouldn't've done it.'

'You still in the union?' Cogan said.

'Nah,' Mitch said. 'I hadda give that up. There's too many, you know what they're doing now? It's the fuckin' PRs, mostly. You hear about it and everybody thinks: it's the niggers. But it's not. New York, maybe some place else it is. But not New York. New York it's PRs. I dunno what the fuck it is. I been there, I been in New York almost twenty years. The whole time I been there, somebody's been howling for something. It's not the niggers, it's the PRs. Those bastards, they come in onna plane, they own the whole fuckin' town all of a sudden. All of a sudden everybody's got to get down and kiss the goddamned PRs' ass. You get yourself a sandwich and there's a hungry PR around, because, of course, there's *always* gonna be a hungry PR around, they're too fuckin' good-looking to go to work or anything, forget your sandwich. There's gonna be some guy from Washington standing around, giving you the hardeyes. "Leave him have the sandwich, Jason. He's a spic and he's entitled." I look around, you look around in New York and all you can see is spics, wall-to-wall spics wiggling their ass. I swear they're all queer. No, I'm selling cars.'

'Jesus,' Cogan said, 'I wouldn't think, it'd pay that good.'

'Doesn't,' Mitch said, 'don't pay for shit. But you're the guy, owns the thing, all right? Now that guy makes out. Guys that've got the same kind of job I have, you really got to hammer ass and get lucky, too, you wanna make a buck. But the guy, he's my wife's uncle, right? I should've married him. Him and me get along fine. So I do all right, and I'm outdoors and you get to go to the meetings and all. It's just for the time being. I go near one of them fuckin' jobs now and everybody's screaming fuckin' bloody murder. I got a record and I got this and I got that, and that asshole in New Jersey, I swear every time the guy picked the phone up he was telling somebody what a hot shit I am, oh, he was a great one. So, you got to wait, it'll die down. It always does. The fuckin' Chinks'll be next. What the fuck, I mean, sooner or later they're probably gonna *have* a fuckin' election and that crazy fuckin' guy that wants to give the world away to somebody, anybody, so long's he's a nigger himself and thinks the niggers oughta own the world, he'll get his ass whipped and then things'll quiet down again. I'll find something.'

The waiter brought two more drinks. He was an elderly man, bent in the formal uniform. 'Where do you have to go for these?' Mitch said. The waiter straightened up and stared at Mitch. 'I said: Where do you have to go for these things?' Mitch said. 'I know it's some place outa the building, here, it's obviously gotta be. You maybe even got to walk a couple blocks, take a cab or something. I was just wondering.'

'No, sir,' the waiter said, 'we only have one man on the service and lunch bars today, and he's very busy. Are the drinks all right?'

'Well,' Mitch said, 'as a matter of fact, no, it's mostly evaporated by the time it gets here.'

'Mitch,' Cogan said. 'Yeah,' he said to the waiter, 'the drinks are all right.'

The waiter went away.

'The next one I'm gonna send in for,' Mitch said. 'They probably got an order blank in a magazine or something, you can mail it in and then when you get here it only takes them about a week to get you what you want.'

'You picked it,' Cogan said.

'The only place in fuckin' Boston I know about, I could remember, for Christ sake,' Mitch said. 'I never come here. You know how many times I come here? I been here, this's the fourth or fifth time I been here in my whole life. I just never come here, is all. Every time I have to go somewhere, it's Detroit, it's Chicago, it's something like that. I was in St. Louis, the last time I hadda go someplace. I just never come here. Guy asked me the other day, I wanna do something. I told him no, I was gonna be out of town. "Jesus," he said, "you going all the way to Brooklyn or something?"'

'You tell him, you're coming up here?' Cogan said.

'For Christ sake, no,' Mitch said. 'I was just saying, I never come up here much. I suppose, when they needed somebody, they usually must've had somebody else they used to call. Course I haven't been doing much except staying away from a lot of things lately anyway. Or things've been staying away from me, anyway.'

'Yeah?' Cogan said.

'Yeah,' Mitch said. He finished his drink. He signaled to the waiter and pointed to his glass. The waiter, slowly, began to move toward the service bar. 'You don't mind if I drink one of them beers while I'm waiting for that guy to make it in from the airport, do you?' Mitch said. He was reaching for a stein of dark.

'No,' Cogan said. 'It'll make you fat, though, I thought you said.'

Mitch drank some of the beer. 'Yeah,' he said. 'First there was that thing on the phones. Jesus, I could've killed that guy. I mean it. I could've found somebody, gimme the okay, I would've done him for nothing. On the fuckin' cuff. Then, then, well, I hadda leave the hall on account of that. And I wasn't feeling good, you know? So I go the doctor, and he gives me the stuff, and he asks me: have I been under some kind of tension or something. Of course not, just gettin' my name in the paper all the time, more'n Rockefeller, I bet, I used to be a guy that could go in and organize something and keep everything going all right, now all of a sudden I don't do nothing but break people's legs and stuff and throw bombs or something at them. I forget what it was. And I'm getting hell from my wife all the time, naturally. No, there's nothing bothering me. And I take the stuff and I get fat and then I got myself a good dose in Saratoga, I was up there with a couple of the guys, and then they grabbed me down in Maryland on that gun thing.'

'What gun thing?' Cogan said.

'I was goin' huntin', for Christ sake,' Mitch said. 'Me and another guy. You know Topper?'

'No,' Cogan said.

Mitch finished the beer. The waiter arrived with the drink. 'You didn't bring him a beer, I bet,' Mitch said.

'No, sir,' the waiter said. 'You only wanted the one, I thought.'

'You thought wrong,' Mitch said. 'Bring him a beer, too. I just drank the man's beer on him.'

'I don't want any more,' Cogan said to the waiter. 'It's all right.'

The waiter nodded.

Mitch shrugged. 'Okay,' he said, 'don't have no more. Yeah. Topper. Nice guy. Lives out on Long Island. We move out there, guy tells me, I should look him up. "Getting old," he says, "still a nice guy." So I do. Likes to fish.'

'I went fishing once,' Cogan said. 'Got onna fuckin' boat. All these guys, drinking beer. I look at the guy. "What is this?" I say. "I can go the ball game, I want to watch guys drinking beer." It was awful. It was rough and all them guys, drinking beer, they all start throwing up. Fuck fishing.'

'This's surf casting, he does,' Mitch said. 'You go out and you stand on the beach and all. It's pretty good.' Mitch drank half of the martini. He belched silently. 'It's just, the only thing wrong with it is, you got to get up too early. But what the fuck, he wants to go. My wife starts in on me. "Jesus Christ," I tell her, "leave me alone, all right?" You ever been shooting geese?'

'No,' Cogan said. 'That's the trouble, I work. I work all night and all day and then I go home and I go to bed. So naturally, I take a few days off, I still live the same way. My wife, now what my wife's always telling me, I'm working too hard. And that's true. See, I had this one operation, and it's all right, but anybody can see what's happening, it's just a matter of time, the state starts taking all kinds of action, and it'll still be there, no question about that, but it's not gonna be as good. So I started, I started up this thing with the cigarettes, and I got that thing going pretty good. Six months after I take it over, it's going like a bat out of hell. So, good, I hadda get a guy and give him some of it, I still supply him but he runs the locations I got west of here and I just take care of the others. So, it's getting better. But it drives her batty, we go some place and we get there and then I can't sleep. I'm not used to going to bed so early, and I stay up and then I sleep late and we can't do nothing. "You're exhausted," she tells me, and I am. But I tried changing it back and forth and I can't do it. I been at it too long. I oughta get into something else, I guess. Better hours.'

'You got to change every so often,' Mitch said. 'That's one of things, the union thing? It went to hell, well, I didn't like it. But I was doing it a long time, I was, in a way I was kind of glad too, you know? That's what Topper says. He's seventy, at least, he doesn't do things any more. He was telling me that. "The trouble with you guys," he says, "you spend your whole life, you're doing the same thing and all you're ever doing's getting old. You've got to keep trying new things." So I listened to him, we're goin' down the Maryland shore, there, a whole bunch of people're just taking over this motel and they're all the right kind of guys, we're gonna hunt geese. So, we go down there, I, there was probably a couple hundred cops around the place? And we've got the shotguns in the trunk. Oh, fuckin' beautiful. "Where're you going? What're you gonna do? Where're you from?" So we don't say anything, naturally, I mean, they done a lot of things but this isn't fuckin' Russia yet, I think, and everybody's standing around and now they're gonna start searching cars. And I'm gonna ask them, they got any warrants or anything, and I'm really gonna do it. Topper takes hold of me. There's four or five of them standing around, I was really afraid he was going to say something. Just shakes his head. Doesn't even do that, really. Topper's all right. I don't say anything.

'So,' Mitch said, 'they open up the cars and there's the shotguns, me and Topper's car. It was Topper's wife's car, actually. Two shotguns right there. I just bought the fuckin' shotgun, for Christ sake. I went down the place and I bought the fuckin' shotgun. I hadda have my wife's uncle sign for it, of course, but I actually went out and paid for the thing. Nobody gave it to me or anything. I never even used it once. Guy looks at them. Then he comes over. Treasury. I'm under arrest. Felon in possession. You think, you think I said a single word to them? No. But what does he say: 'Mister Mitchell,' and then he starts telling me. So, it probably just happened, they know my record and everything. I look at Topper. Nope, they arrest him, too. They know his name. I'm thinking: pretty soon I start asking around, see how come these guys know when I'm gonna take a shit and everything.

' "Just for your information," the guy says to me,' Mitch said, ' "you might be interested to know, we picked you up at the Throg's Neck Bridge this morning. You guys've got to learn some day, stop having these conventions." So there I am. I'm probably gonna go to jail for a fuckin' shotgun I bought in a fuckin' store, I was gonna use to shoot geese with, for Christ sake.'

'Jesus,' Cogan said.

Mitch finished the martini. He signaled to the waiter, pointing to Cogan's empty stein first.

'You're hitting that stuff pretty hard, aren't you, Mitch?' Cogan said.

'I was up all night,' Mitch said. 'I can never sleep, I'm going some place the next day onna plane. Them things make me nervous. Then, I come in like this, I got to sleep before I'm good for anything that day. I'm gonna go the hotel, we finish here, get some sleep. I told the doctor, he was gonna put me back on the cortisone, it started up again after that thing in Maryland, and I said: "No." I don't care what it is, I'll change my pants three times a day if I have to, I got to get rid of this weight I got on me. Only I think, well, Topper feels responsible. And he looks, he's little and he's old and he didn't take a pinch for about thirty years, I think.

So, they're probably gonna both be his shotguns. I was just doing an old man a favor, driving him down there and all.'

'Yeah,' Cogan said, 'but if they don't ...'

'I do time,' Mitch said. 'It's very simple. If they're not his guns, I do time. I did it before. If I have to, I can do it again. They're gonna have to practically turn themselves inside out, get me more'n three even with the rap sheet I got, for that. Oh Jesus, do them guys love arresting you. They just love it. They get some-body, they finally get a guy, they know his name, Jesus Christ, you'd think some of them're little kids. Like to bash them right inna mouth, they like it so much. Bastards. But, big fuckin' deal. I do a year. I don't like it, but shit, that's the way it goes.'

'Rough onna wife, though,' Cogan said. 'That's the one thing, you know, Carol can never get it off of her mind, I might get bagged and have to go to jail. Most of the time she don't give me any shit, except about the way I'm out all the time and everything. But every so often, well, they hooked four guys there and they got them in front the grand jury and they asked them, who's the guy they're looking for, you know? Like you say: the guy, they know who he is. And naturally they don't say anything. And then they get this immunity.'

'They been doing that down in Brooklyn,' Mitch said. 'They got everybody in the slammer, and what'd they do? They wouldn't say anything.'

'Yeah,' Cogan said. 'So, the same thing, they go to jail. And if they don't tell them, which they're naturally not gonna do, they're gonna have to stay there. So they're in the can. And my wife was saying, well, I told her, I said, I'm not big enough. And I'm get-ting out of it anyway, fast as I can. Guys like me, they don't even know I'm around. Those're much bigger guys'n I am. But I can see it. I think, I don't think she could take it, really, something like that happened. Every time they come in and ask for the toll sheets, there, everybody knows, they talk about it the cafeteria. And she gets all worried and everything. "Just promise me one thing, you'll stay away from phones where they know you." So, I do. But I'm almost out of that anyway. I don't think she could take it, really, something like that happened.'

'None of them can,' Mitch said. The waiter delivered the martini and the beer. Mitch drank the beer. He wiped his mouth. He belched, softly. 'The last time, the last time she actually took out the papers. And I didn't blame her. She was a lot younger then. But when we're trying that thing, the last day? The jury's gonna get the case that day. I get up and she's already up. I dunno how long that is, but I was up at five or so to take a leak, and she wasn't in bed then. She says: "Doesn't look good, does it?" Well, what the hell, it didn't. The cop lied on the stand, of course, put me in the place at nine-thirty, it was at least after ten when I got there that night, and the jury believed him, of course. So, I say, no, it didn't. And we go in the bedroom, get dressed. And I'm putting my pants on and I'm watching her, she's getting dressed, I dunno how she does it, the way she drinks and everything, but she always hadda nice body, and I was thinking, you know? Now I'm goin' away again, and she'll start beating the shit out of the sauce and everything, and I *know* she'll play around. Shit, I mean, I don't like the feeling it gives me in the nuts, knowing it, but I wouldn't even ask her, you know? Just because I'm inna can, she's supposed to go without it just like she's inna can with me? So she looks at me. "This's the third time I've had to do this, Harold," she says. She never called me Mitch, and she knows I hate that name.

'"Look," I tell her,' Mitch said, '"you never know what'll

happen." ' He drank some of the martini. ' "What's gonna happen, you never know."

'And she says to me,' Mitch said, ' "Well, you think you know what's gonna happen, and I think it's gonna happen, and I don't know if I can take it again." '

'So it happened,' Mitch said, 'and then the papers come up and I was gonna sign them, let her have what she wants if this's what she wants. She went through it twice. The girl don't owe me nothing. She probably is sick of it. But then, I asked her to come up and see me, and I said: "Margie, look, you know? You want this, you're really sure, you can have it. But what's it gonna get you, huh?" She was, she was thirty-nine, forty, then. "You're still gonna have the kids, you're still gonna have to know, I get out, I'm not gonna be in here forever and you're gonna have to see me when I see them. I'm not gonna stop coming around, seeing them. And, we been together a long time. Unless, unless you really got somebody else you really got to have, okay?" See, I knew she was seeing this guy. So, she don't answer me. And I say: "Look, do this for me. Don't do nothing now. You had, you know, when I come out last time, we're both a lot younger then and all, and you hadda decide then." And she looks at me: "And you promised me then," she says, "you promised me then, you were all through. And here I am again, and you'll promise me now, again, and I'll wait five years and get six more, and then you'll do something again." '

' "Margie," I said,' Mitch said, ' "what can I say to you? I know. You're right. But all I'm asking, you can do, wait'll I come out again. Because, I dunno who the guy is," ' Mitch said, 'and I did, of course. I knew about it two days after she was with him the first time. I don't blame him, either. "I oughta at least, you oughta at least do this for me: I oughta be around the same's he is. Because we always got along all right." And she starts crying and shaking her head, and I really thought. But she didn't. And it was all right. I think, you know, you know anything about kids? Probably not.' Mitch finished the martini.

'You're not having any more of those things,' Cogan said. 'You'll fall on your ass if you do.'

'I can handle it,' Mitch said. 'I was drinking before you got out of your father's cock. Don't tell me what I do.' He signaled the waiter. He pointed twice at Cogan's empty stein. 'Nobody knows anything about kids,' Mitch said. 'But, it's really hard on the kids. I think it was that, probably, what did it to them, the way they hadda be and all. They're no good. Oh, they're good enough. My daughter's all right. But my son, he won't have nothing to do with me. And I think, this's the funny part, all right? I think it probably was that, that she did it for, and it probably would've been better for them if she didn't. I think that's why she drinks so much, now.'

'I thought she was all right,' Cogan said, 'we're down in Florida, there.'

'She was,' Mitch said. 'Look, when I was down there she was all right. When I *went* down there. She really was. I believed it. But see, that was the first time she was all right, and since then, I seen what happened. I talked to some guys, everybody that's got somebody like that, and the first time they shake it, you know, you always think they shook it and that's the end of it. *They* always think that, they think that themselves. But they never do. Nobody like that's ever all right again, ever. I came back, there, I was home about a month and we're going at it left and right, this and that, well, look, I dunno what it is, you know? But I wasn't sorry I hadda come up here, lemme put it that way. She was going at it again. They can't stay away from it when they get like that. The best they can do is, they can stay away from it for a while. I think something finally happens to them. I go away, I go away on this thing again, she'll go down the slide once and for all before they get the gray suit on me. And this time, boy, I find that out, I get the papers again from her, this time I sign them. It's too fuckin' rough for me.'

The waiter brought two steins of dark. He set them both in front of Mitch. Cogan said: 'Check.' The waiter nodded. Mitch drank half of the first stein.

'It's a terrible amount of shit, you got to go through,' Cogan said.

'Hey,' Mitch said, 'look, you know? What can you do? Do the best you can. Think I'm gonna leave the country like some fuckin' draft dodger or something? Fuck that. It don't make no difference anyway. What're we doing?'

'We got this,' Cogan said, 'we got two guys. There's actually four guys, but one of them's probably not around and I'm not sure, we really want the other one. So, we got two guys, for sure, and one of them knows me, so here you are.'

'Well,' Mitch said, 'am I doing a double or what? These guys hang around or something?'

'Uh uh,' Cogan said. 'Well, I mean, you wanna take the double, it's all right with me, you think you can handle it. You need that?'

'I could use the dough,' Mitch said. 'I'm gonna have to try this thing and it's gonna cost me my left ball to do it. You know where the pricks indicted me? Maryland. Not in New York, Maryland. So I got to go down there and everything, and fart around in some motel, and it's gonna mean two lawyers, my guy, that looks like he never got out the garment district in his life, Solly's a great guy, but if a guy ever looked like a sharp New York Jew, it's Solly.

154

And then the other guy, some guy that probably wears overalls or something, so they don't hook me just because I got Solly. Yeah, I need dough.'

'Well,' Cogan said, 'you want the two of them, it's fine with me.'

'I oughta take you up on it,' Mitch said. 'But I think, I'm not supposed to be up here, you know? I'm restricted, New York and Maryland and that stuff, I'm supposed, I'm not supposed, go any place else unless I ask them. Well, I didn't ask. So I probably shouldn't hang around here any longer'n I absolutely have to. And, two's risky, too. No, I better stick with the one.'

'Okay,' Cogan said. 'Now, here's the thing: that's gonna be the guy that knows me. Well, he don't know me, but he's one of the few guys that probably knows who I am, all right? He knows me and he knows Dillon, and if he hears anything, he's gonna figure, he's gonna be waiting for Dillon or me. So, he's the one.'

'He got friends?' Mitch said.

'One of the guys that we might do,' Cogan said. 'He's a kid, he could be around. He's a fairly tough kid, too. The other kid, he's the guy that's apparently not around. So, there might be the one.'

'We gonna do anything about him?' Mitch said.

'Right now,' Cogan said, 'it depends. I honestly don't know. See, the other guy, I got him in mind for tonight. And a lot depends, what happens after that.'

'The fuck happened, anyway?' Mitch said.

'One of them fuckin' *things*,' Cogan said. 'There's this guy, got a game, all right? And he got some guys, one time, knock it over for him, and then, well, he got away with it. So, and then everybody says: "Okay." Then this other guy comes along, and he gets these two kids, and they go in and they knock it over again, right? They think he's gonna get blamed for it again. That's the guy I'm doing. I'm gonna put his light out tonight, I figure, things go all right.'

'Dumb shit,' Mitch said. He finished the first stein.

'Right,' Cogan said. The waiter brought the check. Cogan paid it.

'On your way back,' Mitch said, 'you think you're gonna be in this neighborhood again this year, you can bring me two more.'

'No, you can't,' Cogan said to the waiter. He took the second stein. 'I'm gonna drink this, even if I don't want it. He's drinking coffee. Bring the man nice black coffee.'

'Hey,' Mitch said.

'Hey yourself,' Cogan said. 'I'm gonna have to talk to you. I don't wanna have to go down, see you inna fuckin' tank. Too many guys around down there, listening to other people's business. Coffee for you.'

'I won't be able to sleep,' Mitch said.

'Watch television,' Cogan said.

'I probably won't,' Mitch said. 'You're gonna line something up for me, instead.'

'You gotta have that?' Cogan said.

'Shit,' Mitch said. 'I'm not working tonight, right?'

'Nope,' Cogan said.

'And I'm probably not working tomorrow night, either,' Mitch said. 'We got to set this thing up, and all. Who's gonna help me?'

'I got a kid,' Cogan said. 'He's not the sharpest thing I ever seen, but he'll do what you tell him. You want him to drive, he'll drive. Anything.'

'Is he gonna fuck up?' Mitch said. 'Never mind what somebody tells him, does he fuck up?'

'Look,' Cogan said, 'this kid'd tear a fuckin' car in half with his bare hands, you asked him. He's very dependable. But you got to tell him. You tell him, he'll do it. He'll go through a fuckin' building, he's got to.'

'I personally,' Mitch said, 'I'd rather have a guy that'd see the building and go around it. I can't afford, I don't want no guy that's gonna go on no fuckin' rampage the minute I let him out of my sight. You sure you can't come in on this?'

'Look,' Cogan said, 'the guy's name's Johnny Amato. I know him. I did, he wanted Dillon to do something for him once, and Dillon couldn't do it. So Dillon told him, if it was all right, he'd ask me, and the guy said: "Yeah." So I did it, and he paid me. He knows me.'

'How much does this kid know?' Mitch said.

'Kenny?' Cogan said. 'Kenny knows nothing. I didn't tell him nothing. He don't know you're in town. He knew it, it wouldn't mean nothing to him.'

'I don't want him,' Mitch said.

The waiter brought Cogan's change and the coffee.

'I don't want that, either,' Mitch said.

The waiter left.

'I didn't say you wanted it,' Cogan said.

'I don't want no fuckin' nutcakes, either,' Mitch said.

'Well,' Cogan said, 'look, I mean, you got to tell me what you want, then, right? Because I don't know.'

'Where is this guy?' Mitch said.

'Quincy,' Cogan said. 'Wollaston, actually.'

'I don't know where the fuck that is,' Mitch said.

'I can show you,' Cogan said.

'But he knows you,' Mitch said. 'Great. Look, this other guy, the one you're doing?'

'Yeah,' Cogan said.

'Do him,' Mitch said, 'and the way I get it, that's gonna do something to the guy I'm supposed to hit.'

'Got to,' Cogan said.

'Gonna make him relax, or something,' Mitch said.

'I think,' Cogan said.

'Okay, then,' Mitch said. 'So, we got to give him a chance to relax then, haven't we? And you got to get me somebody that can drive a car without running into things, and also you got to get me something. You haven't got anything yet, I assume.'

'I was gonna ask you what you wanted,' Cogan said.

'Good,' Mitch said, 'forty-five Military Police. I never use nothing else.'

'Okay,' Cogan said.

'If you're the guy that's starting it,' Mitch said, 'it's a great thing. One of them. And a guy that can do things. How long's that gonna take you?'

'Day or so,' Cogan said.

'And a car,' Mitch said.

'Still a day or so,' Cogan said.

'And where he's gonna be,' Mitch said.

'Same thing,' Cogan said.

'You know something?' Mitch said. 'I don't think you can do it that fast.'

'I can,' Cogan said.

'Well,' Mitch said, 'then I think you're not gonna and I don't care if you can or not. Now, this's, we're gonna do this, this is Thursday. We're gonna do him Saturday night. That's when we're gonna do it. You guys're all half-assed up here. You don't take the time to think about things. I do.'

'Always glad to meet a guy, you can learn something from,' Cogan said.

'I been at this a long time,' Mitch said. 'I messed up some things, but never one of these. Now, that leaves me tonight and tomorrow night. Who's gonna see me tonight?'

'I can't promise nothing special,' Cogan said.

'Don't like fuckin', is that it?' Mitch said.

'Never paid for it, anyway,' Cogan said.

'Well, company's what I want,' Mitch said. 'You get me some company for tonight. I'll take it from there. Fourteen-o-nine. I'm in the tower, all right?'

'That,' Cogan said, 'I'll do the best I can for you. That's something you're gonna have to decide.'

12

'He's not walking right,' Gill said. He wore a dark blue tanker jacket and sat opposite Cogan in the Hayes Bickford across the street from the Lobster Tail.

'Of course he's not walking right,' Cogan said. 'He's hurt. He's all beat to shit.'

'It takes him a long time to do something,' Gill said. 'I seen him, he was getting out of his car. It takes him a long time.'

'He's all taped up,' Cogan said.

'He's sure slow,' Gill said.

'He don't feel good,' Cogan said. 'You wouldn't feel good, either.'

'What're we gonna do, Jack?' Gill said.

'You're gonna drive the car,' Cogan said. 'Never mind thinking about what I'm gonna do. You just think about what you're gonna do.'

'I'm gonna get some money,' Gill said.

'Five hundred,' Cogan said, 'same as always, five hundred. You don't fuck anything up.'

'I ever fuck anything up with you?' Kenny said.

'Kenny,' Cogan said, 'the world's full of guys that never fucked up, and then they did something and they fucked up once and they're doing time. So this's no night to start, not when I'm with you. What'd you get for a car?'

'Olds,' Gill said. 'Last year's Four-four-two. Nice car.'

'Don't get attached to it,' Cogan said. 'You got everything in it, I gave you?'

'Sure,' Gill said.

'The way I gave it to you and all,' Cogan said.

'Yeah,' Gill said.

'Okay,' Cogan said, 'all you gotta do is, you got to drive.'

'Who is this guy?' Gill said.

'Don't matter,' Cogan said.

'No,' Gill said, 'I mean, really. Who is this guy? This the guy Steve and Barry beat up?'

'Kenny,' Cogan said.

'I didn't mean nothing,' Gill said. 'I was just wondering. I was, there was this guy, really got beat up, he was running a card game. And this guy, he's hurt, I was wondering if it was the same guy.'

'Who told you about the guy with the card game, Kenny,' Cogan said.

'Jack,' Gill said, 'like I said, I was just wondering. I didn't mean nothing. What'd he do with the card game?'

'He had a couple guys come in and knock it over,' Cogan said.

'Oh,' Gill said. 'See, well, I couldn't understand it. Steve and Barry.'

'You figured I should've asked you,' Cogan said.

'I could've used the money, Jack,' Gill said.

'You can always use the money,' Cogan said. 'Thing of it is, and I didn't ask them, incidentally, you got that?'

'Sure,' Gill said.

'The thing needed two guys,' Cogan said. 'That's why you didn't get called.'

'I could've got another guy,' Gill said. 'I could've got the guy I had with me onna dogs.'

'Uh huh,' Cogan said, 'well, okay, Kenny. Next time I need two guys, I'll call you.'

'He would've been all right,' Kenny said. 'He's a good guy. Only, I don't think he's gonna hang around much now.'

'Okay, Kenny,' Cogan said, 'you just keep things in mind, I need two guys some time, I'll maybe call you first and if you can get me a guy, I'll use you. Okay?'

'Okay,' Kenny said. 'See, I was just thinking, was all, Jack.'

'That's your weak spot, Kenny,' Cogan said. 'Never mind it. Just do like I tell you, everything'll be all right.'

'Does he know?' Gill said.

'Nah,' Cogan said, 'he oughta, but he probably doesn't. I don't think so, no.'

Wearing a gray and red tattersall coat, Mark Trattman, his hands in his pockets, emerged from the Lobster Tail alone. The attendant in the snorkel coat started walking down the street.

'Son of a bitch,' Cogan said. 'Didn't score tonight for a change.'

'He was drinking his drink through them little plastic things you're supposed to steer them with,' Gill said. 'Those little green and white things.'

'Yeah,' Cogan said. He set his coffee cup down. 'Where's the fuckin' car?'

'Around the side,' Gill said. 'I thought you said—'

'Never mind what you thought I said,' Cogan said. 'Move your big dumb ass. The guy's going home.'

'I don't get it,' Gill said.

'Neither's he, tonight,' Cogan said. 'Never again, either. Come on, for Christ sake, we're gonna get home early for a change.'

The yellow 4-4-2 trailed Trattman's tan Coupe de Ville through eight consecutive green lights on Commonwealth Avenue, west-bound. Cogan rode in the back, sitting behind the driver's seat. He kept his hands down, out of sight.

'Jesus,' Gill said, 'he's pretty good at this. He hits them all, just's they turn.'

'He knows the speed,' Cogan said. 'They're set for nineteen or twenty miles an hour, I think it is. Something like that. He does it all the time, for Christ sake. He oughta.'

'Jack,' Gill said, 'what if, what if he hasn't gotta stop?'

'We'll take him home and put him to fuckin' bed then,' Cogan said. 'Just keep after him, Kenny, and remember what I told you about thinking. Don't worry about nothing. Just you change lanes now and then and everything'll be all right.'

On the long hill at the synagogue, the Cadillac swung into the right lane and the brake lights came on as it approached the intersection of Chestnut Hill Avenue. The traffic light was red. A streetcar moved west toward Lake Street beyond the intersection.

'Middle lane, Kenny,' Cogan said. 'There's three lanes, it goes to three lanes up here. Take the middle.' He began to straighten up in the back seat. He leaned over and cranked down the right rear passenger window with his left hand.

The 4-4-2 approached the Cadillac quickly off the left rear.

'Right up even,' Cogan said, 'nice and smooth.'

The traffic light remained red. There were no other cars. The traffic lights on Chestnut Hill Avenue turned yellow.

'Right up next to him,' Cogan said. 'Then a little bit ahead. Put me right next to him, Kenny. Atta boy.'

Gill stopped the 4-4-2 with the open right rear window even with the driver's window of the Cadillac. Trattman looked lazily at the car. He looked back at the traffic light.

Cogan ran the 30-06 Savage semi-automatic rifle out the rear window of the 4-4-2 and fired five times. The first bullet crazed Trattman's window. Trattman lurched off to the right and was snubbed up abruptly. Cogan said: 'Good for you, Markie, always wear your seat belt.'

The Cadillac started to creep forward as Cogan finished firing, Trattman bent forward at an angle over the passenger seat. When Gill swung the 4-4-2 left on Chestnut Hill Avenue, the Cadillac was halfway across; it ran up against the curbstone as the lights in the apartments at the intersection started to come on.

13

Russell, carrying a brown-paper bag, came out of the Arlington Street MBTA station just before six o'clock and turned off Arlington at St. James. At the newsstand on the corner the old man was cutting wire on bundles of the *Globe*. Two men in business suits waited in a light green Ford sedan at the newsstand, the passenger with his head and left hand out of the window, offering change. The driver watched Russell turn right on St. James. Holding the microphone in his right hand, the driver spoke into it: 'All units, this is unit three. He finally made it.'

Russell crossed the street, pausing for a Greyhound bus to pull into the terminal parking lot, in from Bangor. The driver of the third Yellow Cab in line at the terminal spoke into his microphone: 'Unit four to all units. I got him now. He's on the sidewalk. He's about to enter the station.'

The light green Ford started moving toward the next

intersection. It turned right at Stuart Street and went the wrong way up behind the terminal.

In the station a man in a light blue private security force uniform stood at the top of the stairs, his back to the doors, watching the reflection of the entrance doors in the glass of the windows of the lounge. He wore a hearing aid button in his right ear.

Russell came through the doors, into the terminal.

The man in the light blue suit bent his neck to the left and talked out of the left side of his mouth into the small rectangular bulge in his uniform shirt. 'This is unit seven. All units converge.'

The two men in business suits left the light green Ford and went to the doors of the terminal on the easterly side. The driver got out of the cab and went to the door on the westerly side. Four men got out of a blue Dodge Polara in front of the terminal. Two moved to the front of the terminal. One went to join the cab driver on the westerly side. One joined the men from the light green Ford on the easterly side. Two baggage handlers, each wearing a hearing aid button, stepped back from the baggage check-in and stood near the doors at the back of the terminal. One of the ticket sellers, in a white shirt, stepped out from behind the counter, moving slowly.

Russell paused to let the ticket seller walk in front of him. The ticket seller roused a drunk, asleep on the bench. He began to usher the drunk toward the easterly doors. After Russell had his back to them, the drunk required less assistance.

Russell went to the baggage lockers on the westerly side of the terminal.

The man in the security force uniform watched from the top of the stairs. He spoke again. 'Unit seven to all units. West side, west side.'

Russell inserted the key to locker 352 and turned it.

The men from the light green Ford entered the terminal through the easterly doors.

Russell opened the locker and took out a box wrapped in brown paper. He opened the bag and put the box in. Leaving the locker door ajar, he turned toward the front of the terminal. He carried the bag in his left hand.

The driver of the cab entered through the westerly door. The two men in the baggage room went out into the passenger area of the terminal. The men from the Polara came in through the front doors and the man in the security force uniform turned slowly away from the front doors as Russell approached them.

The men from the light green Ford walked up behind Russell, one on each side. When they were half a pace behind him, they took him firmly by the elbows. Russell's body sagged.

The man on Russell's right said: 'Bureau Narcotics. You're under arrest.' He had a chrome-plated forty-five automatic in his right hand. He stuck the barrel close to Russell's face.

The man on Russell's left had handcuffs in his left hand. He stepped backward without letting go of Russell's arm and swung it behind Russell. He locked one cuff on Russell's left wrist and took the bag from him. He pulled Russell's right arm back and locked the wrist into the cuff. He patted Russell down. He shook his head.

The man with the automatic said: 'You're pretty fuckin' obvious, my friend. Matter of fact, you're so fuckin' obvious I was afraid you'd forget where you left the stuff, or lose the key or something. *You've* got a right to remain silent. Anything you say can and *will* be used against you at a trial in a fuckin' court of law. You got a right to an *attorney*, and if you can't *afford* an attorney, us long-suffering good and noble taxpayers'll go out and treat you to the best fuckin' shyster we can find. I think you also got a right to have your head tested, and in your case, I think you oughta, see if there's anything in it at all.'

'I wanna make my phone call,' Russell said. The agents urged him toward the door.

'They got a real nice phone in the Marshal's office, my friend,' the agent said. 'It's a great little instrument. You can call any place in the country on it. That's if you know how to dial. If you don't know how to dial, we'll teach you how to do it. If you call long distance, we'll put it on your bill.'

'Thanks,' Russell said.

'Buddy,' the agent said, 'don't thank me. I think you're gonna be surprised when you get that bill. You're goin' in for all day on this one, my friend. Unless of course your friend down there in New York figured out how stupid you really are, and sold you quinine or something. All's well that ends well, right, my friend?'

'Shut up,' Russell said.

The agents escorted Russell out of the terminal, into the darkness.

'That's not one of your rights, my friend,' the agent said. 'That's one of my rights. But I got a little deal for you, all right, my friend? Any time you wanna talk, just tell me, and I'll shut up. Just say the word and you have got the fuckin' floor.'

'Fuck you,' Russell said.

The Polara made a U-turn on St. James and pulled up in front of the terminal.

The agent dug the barrel of the automatic into Russell's rib cage. 'That, my friend,' he said in a soft voice, 'is not the kind of talk I meant. People've been known to fall down a lot getting in and out

168

of cars and so forth when they talk like that. Got it?' Russell said nothing. 'And another thing, my friend,' the agent said. 'Not only are you stupid but you stink. I think you're gonna get twenty years and a bath. I dunno which you need more.'

14

'The stupid shit,' Frankie said. He sat in Amato's office. 'You know who he picks to call, of course. Me. Only he don't remember I moved, so he calls Sandy, and he got her up and she's all pissed and she calls me and give me a whole ration of shit and then I got to call him and I hadda girl with me. And of course I got to give my name to them, they won't let anybody else talk to him.'

'That's good,' Amato said.

'Yeah,' Frankie said. 'Oh, I'm gonna really enjoy this, I can tell. Wants me to come down and see him. "Yeah," I said, "sure, Russell, and I won't have a hundred ballbusters following me around for the rest of my life if I do that, either. No thanks. I didn't have nothing to do with it and I told you what was gonna happen and you wouldn't listen to me."'

'"Did you tell them?" he says to me,' Frankie said. '"Are you the fuckin' bastard that told them?"'

' "Russell," I said,' Frankie said, ' "nobody hadda tell them. You told them yourself. What am I gonna tell cops anything for? Tell me that, huh? You wanna blame somebody, blame yourself." That calmed him down some. Well, will I make bail for him? "Depends," I said. See, he hasn't got no money left. Spent it on his problem, which I don't think they're probably gonna let him go out and sell, now. "What's the bail?" Just what you'd expect, his record and a pound of that stuff. One hundred thousand dollars.'

'Ten K from you,' Amato said.

'Well,' Frankie said, 'there's guys that'll write one for five per cent if you wanna handle some things for them now and then, but onna guy like him I doubt you could get it even from one of them. But either way, it's too much, and besides, I tell him, "Keep in mind, I just got out of the can myself. Where'd I get all that bread?" No, I said I'd call somebody for him, but that's all, he can make his own deal. "You ask me," I said, "I don't even think that's gonna do it for you, though. You raise the hundred, they'll go to double surety or two hundred or something. Those guys aren't gonna let you out. Forget it." '

'So that's what he tells me,' Frankie said, 'and then he says: "Frankie, if I don't get out of here, I'm gonna tell them you were in it with me." '

'Nice guy,' Amato said.

'Ah,' Frankie said, 'he was all pissed off. I don't blame him. And what the fuck's he gonna tell them? I said: "Russell, get off the pot, all right? You bring me into this, I'll tell them everything you told me about Goat-ass stealing that other stuff, and all the dogs and the insurance thing you had with Kenny onna car and everything. So don't hand me that shit." He'll be all right. It's just, he's looking at a lot of time. You can't blame him. I asked a guy, he said his guess is, probably eight, ten, something like that. So naturally that means, they probably told him guys've been getting fifteen or so, maybe more.

'Them guys,' Frankie said, 'I mean, they are *bad*. This kid I talked to, he said they come at you from just about every place at once. "They tell you," he said, "you don't have to say nothing to them. But that sure don't stop them from saying something to you. They toss you in New York," he said, "it's gonna take them, always, three or four hours, before you can see a judge, and all the time they're *talking* to you. I think them guys've got cassettes in them. 'You're a lost dude this time. You're gonna go in and you're never gonna come out again. You're crazy, that's all. We know you're not in it alone. You better talk about it.'" So, he was probably pissing his pants when he called me. So I told him: "Russell, I tell you what: I'll get you a lawyer. That's all I can do for you."'

'The fuck's a lawyer gonna do for him?' Amato said.

'He's gonna do it for me,' Frankie said. 'He's gonna get Russell off my back. He wanted Mike Zinna.'

'I doubt if you can get him Mike,' Amato said. 'I doubt if Mike'll touch him.'

'Oh, for Christ sake,' Frankie said. 'Of course I can't get him Mike. I can't afford Mike, I couldn't get Mike for myself. And Mike, Mike couldn't do nothing for him. What's he gonna do, the guy's alone and he's got it in his hands? Make it disappear? What Russell really needs is a magician. No, I got him Toby.'

'I dunno Toby,' Amato said.

'That's because you never had nothing to do with junk,' Frankie said. 'When they grab you with the junk, you call Toby and you pay him no more'n a grand and he gets you as good a deal as anybody could. The cops all know him. He's cheap and all the good anybody can do for Russell, Toby'll do it, and without going all apeshit and telling the guy to give them the names of everybody he ever saw.

'Added to which,' Frankie said, 'there's certain things Toby won't do, and that's good for me. Because Russell's gonna want something else, I figure.'

'Somebody hit the guy he thinks put him in,' Amato said.

'Right,' Frankie said. 'So, all right, I'm a bastard, but there's no way inna world he's gonna be able, get Toby to tell me that, and I'm not personally gonna go down and see him.'

'Where is he?' Amato said.

'Charles Street,' Frankie said.

'You'll get the message, then,' Amato said.

'I don't object to hearing it,' Frankie said. 'You hear it, you can always say, well, what the fuck, I wouldn't go around and do something like that on what I heard. No, if the guy asked me, I'd have to tell him something, I guess, and I don't wanna do that, you know? I like Russell. He was all right to me, and I told him, not to do this. But shit, Goat-ass just did what he wanted, he went out and stole four pounds of procaine or something like that, and I suppose some fuckin' cop was bright enough, starts wondering who wants pounds of that stuff and that was it for Russell. Goat-ass didn't do anything. And besides, who the fuck am I? I didn't, I don't know anybody.'

'I see where Trattman knows a couple guys or so, though,' Amato said.

'That poor bastard,' Frankie said.

'Well,' Amato said, 'I mean, it wasn't like, you didn't expect it or something.'

'Sure,' Frankie said. 'But, you know, when it didn't happen, and

Russell was telling me all that stuff there, then I was scared shit-less, it wasn't gonna happen. I thought it was gonna happen to me. That don't mean, well, yeah, I'm glad it happened to him. But, I still wish it didn't even happen to him, you know? Didn't have to. Like Russell. I knew this was gonna happen to Russell. I told him. But the fuck, I know the guy. And I can't do nothing to help him. I don't know anybody.'

'He took his chances,' Amato said.

'Sure,' Frankie said, 'and now he's gonna take his time. And you're taking your chances and I'm taking my chances and we're gonna do this thing, sooner or later, and probably they're not gonna get us this time, either. But I was thinking about it, right? Suppose, me and Dean go in the place, all of a sudden we got all kinds of cops around. Who do I call? Who do I call, that's not gonna give me the same kind of shit I give Russell? You know why Russell called me? Because, who else's he got to call? And it's the same thing. If we get grabbed in there, Dean calls Sandy. And what do I do? Have him tell her, get me somebody too? I can't call you, for Christ sake. They'd be waiting for that. I, we haven't got no friends, either. You look at it, you and me and Russell're in exactly the same position, except he's in it now and we're not in it yet.'

'Well, Jesus,' Amato said, 'I mean, this was your idea and every-thing. It isn't like, I came around and saw you on this one. Shit, you're afraid of it, forget it. Won't piss me off any. I just went down there and I did, I did what you wanted. I haven't got no invest-ment in this. I made almost four thousand yesterday alone. I can do without it.'

'Won for a change,' Frankie said.

'Yeah,' Amato said, 'I kind of liked it too. Broke even about, the first part of the week. I got fifteen hundred or so Thursday after and then last night, another twenty-five onna Knicks. Knicks're gonna take it, this time.'

'Yeah,' Frankie said. 'John, you told me it was gonna snow in the winter, I'd go out and bet against it, you know that?'

'Nice when you win, though,' Amato said. 'I figure, after what I been through, I'm gonna be winning pretty good when I start.'

'I figure,' Frankie said, 'I'm never gonna start. I'm gonna stick to things I can figure out.'

'Well,' Amato said, 'what is it, then?'

'How does it look?' Frankie said.

'It looks good to me,' Amato said. 'It's nice and dark, they backed the block up to where they put the fill and there's a lot of brush and stuff there and signs on the roof that'll cover you when you're up on the roof. It's brick in front, which don't matter, and it's cinderblock in back. The roof's flat. Looks like tar and pebbles, some kind of cheap shit. I'd go in through the roof. There's a grocery store on one side and a place that sells glasses on the other side and I suppose you could go in through there. But I wouldn't. I'd go the roof. The guys in there in the daytimes're those dopes from Northeast Protective that couldn't see a hockey game in Boston Garden. The cops, I didn't do the cops yet. Northeast always works on two, three hour schedules because they don't hire enough guys. But if you don't want to do it, it's okay.'

'John,' Frankie said, 'it's not this job. That's what I'm trying to tell you. It's not this one and it's not gonna be the next one, either, that's giving me the yikes. It's just, ah, shit, I dunno what it is. I don't like having guys after me, you know? I don't care who they're working for, I don't like having guys after me.'

15

The black girl, lanky, arched her spine and bent her arms behind her to fasten her bra.

'The first one?' Mitch said. 'She wasn't bad. She wasn't good but she wasn't bad, either. She was all right. Seemed like she was in an awful hurry, though.'

'Well, after all,' Cogan said, 'it was probably pretty short notice for her and all.'

The black girl adjusted her breasts in the bra cups. Then she walked up behind Cogan's chair on the apricot rug and used the heel of her left hand to touch his right shoulder. 'My dress, honey,' she said, 'you're sittin' on my dress.' Cogan moved forward without turning his head. The black girl pulled the white dress out from under him. She put it on over her head, her feet splayed on the rug.

'Shit,' Mitch said, 'its not that. It's the same thing as it is with everything else. Nobody does anything right any more.'

Cogan laughed.

'I mean it,' Mitch said. He picked up the glass on the end table next to his chair. 'This's empty,' he said, looking at it. 'Want one?'

'Too early for me,' Cogan said.

'Early?' Mitch said. He stood up in his tee shirt and shorts. 'After noon.'

'Still too early,' Cogan said. 'You go ahead if you want, though.'

'I'm gonna,' Mitch said. He went into the bathroom.

The black girl arched her back again to zip the dress.

'Honey,' she said, walking around in front of Cogan and stooping, back-to, 'could you zip me up?'

'No,' Cogan said.

Mitch ran water in the bathroom. 'Screwing's no different'n anything else,' he said.

'You bastard,' she said, straightening up. She turned and looked at Cogan. 'I thought you were kidding.'

'I never kid,' Cogan said. He inclined his head toward the bathroom. 'Get your trick to do it.'

Mitch came out of the bathroom, the glass full of dark Scotch and water. 'Nobody gives a good shit any more,' he said. 'You ask somebody to do something and you're willing to pay for it, and they say they'll do it and then they about half do it.'

The girl backed up to Mitch. 'Zip my dress, honey,' she said. 'Your nice friend there wouldn't do it.'

Mitch zipped the dress. 'They still want all the money, though, bet your ass on that. No half money, no sir. All the money.' He went back to the chair, sipping from the glass. 'Half the job. Pisses me off.'

The black girl sat down on the bed and put on her red shoes.

'For a guy that's been having himself a regular party for three days or so,' Cogan said, 'you sure bitch and moan a lot.'

'I've been paying for it,' Mitch said. 'I been paying for it myself. I can bitch about it if I want. You know this broad, this Polly?'

The black girl stood up and straightened her dress. She looked at Mitch. 'Honey?'

'Onna bureau,' Mitch said. He drank. 'Wallet's onna bureau.'

The black girl walked across the room, rotating her hips.

'Everybody knows Polly,' Cogan said.

'That's what the broad you sent up said,' Mitch said.

The black girl picked up the wallet.

'There's a hundred and seventy-three bucks in that,' Mitch said. 'When I get up I wanna find a hundred and forty-eight, got that?'

'*Oh*-kay,' the girl said. She removed currency, counted it and put some back in the wallet. She put the wallet down. She picked up the shiny red shoulder bag from the bureau, opened it and put the money in. 'No tip, Honey?' she said.

'No tip,' Mitch said.

'Because you know, Honey,' she said, 'I got to give all this to my man. Girl needs something for herself now and then.'

'No tip,' Mitch said.

'You're the original sport,' Cogan said.

'Fuck her,' Mitch said. He drank again. 'This's afternoon. She's, this one's gravy, right, *Honey?*'

'It's better'n filing,' the girl said.

'I wouldn't know about that,' Mitch said. 'I never did no filing.'

The girl walked toward the door. 'Well,' she said, 'it's not *much* better'n filing, some times. But it's, it's *mostly* better. Some times, you know, you get an old guy, and then it's just faster.' She opened the door.

'You know, Honey,' Mitch said, 'some day some old bastard you just milked, he might decide to carve you up some, talking like that. How'd you like that?'

'Jesus,' the girl said in the doorway, 'I don't *know*. You think I'd *come?*'

'If you could, you might,' Mitch said. 'Probably not, is what I think.'

'Fuck you,' the girl said closing the door.

'Which,' Mitch said, 'is pretty much what I had in mind when I had her come up here. Christ you got some funny gash in Boston. I hadda practically talk her into it. That Polly, there? Same thing. Nothing but french. "For Christ sake," I say, "I wanna get laid. Isn't that what you do?"'

'No, it's not,' Cogan said. 'Any guy you asked could've told you that. *I* could've told you that.'

'You didn't, though,' Mitch said.

'Well, you didn't ask me,' Cogan said. 'Wasn't me that had her come up here. That broad I sent, she was all right, I assume? The guy said she's all right.'

'No more'n that,' Mitch said. 'I couldn't get over it. I said to her: "Whaddaya mean, french? I happen to like fucking. Who's hiring who, here?" Didn't make no difference at all. You can feel her up, you can finger-fuck her, but you can't fuck her. For Christ sake. A fuckin' blow job.'

'It's supposed to be a great blow job,' Cogan said.

'When you wanna get laid,' Mitch said, 'there's no such thing as a great blow job. She's telling me, guys spend two, three hundred a night for what she does. Is that true?'

'I guess it used to be,' Cogan said.

'Yeah,' Mitch said, 'well, you know what I think? I think you're all nuts, letting broads get away with that.'

'She's supposed to be afraid of the clap,' Cogan said.

'Yeah,' Mitch said, 'well, okay. That line of work, I don't think you oughta be able to say like that, but I didn't have no luck with her. She, she still didn't fuck anybody that I could tell you about. Her teeth fall out, boy, she's gonna be the hit of the world. But not me. You know something? I'll tell you something.' Mitch finished his drink. 'I haven't had a real piece of ass since I was in Florida.'

'That was one fine-lookin' broad you had down there,' Cogan said.

'Sunny,' Mitch said. 'That was Sunny. I suppose you fucked her too, after I was gone.'

'Mitch,' Cogan said, 'when me and Dillon got there that night, she was with you. When we left, you're still there and, wasn't she still with you? You're there, what was it?'

'Three weeks,' Mitch said.

'Three weeks,' Cogan said. 'And I was there five days, inna middle. How the fuck'm I gonna do that?'

'I dunno,' Mitch said. He picked up the glass. 'Empty again.' He got up. 'Sure you won't join me?'

'Not late enough yet, either,' Cogan said.

Mitch went into the bathroom. Cogan heard ice go into the glass. He did not hear water running. 'Sammy did it,' Mitch said from the bathroom.

'The guy from Detroit,' Cogan said. 'Sharp-looking little ginzo.'

'Sammy's Jewish,' Mitch said.

'Okay,' Cogan said. 'I didn't mean anything.'

'No trouble,' Mitch said. 'He looks like a ginzo. I wished he was.

But he's Jewish. All the years I known that guy, he still did it. The son of a bitch.'

Cogan heard water running in the bathroom. Mitch emerged with a dark Scotch and water. He was wiping his mouth with the back of his left hand. 'It's my own stupid fault,' he said. 'The night before I'm leaving, we're having dinner and he comes over, I introduce them and everything. I don't know why this bothers me, you know that?'

'No,' Cogan said.

Mitch sat down. He put the glass on the end table. 'I mean, I know. When I'm there, I'm there and she's with me. When I leave, you're there, and she's with you.'

'She wasn't with me,' Cogan said.

'I didn't mean you,' Mitch said. 'I mean: any guy. Anybody that's there, she's with him. You leave, she's not with you any more.'

'Oh,' Cogan said.

'See,' Mitch said, 'that's what I mean. I know that. I give her, well, last year, I'm down there, I was only there two weeks. No, three weeks. Anyway, that's how many nights?'

'Twenty-one,' Cogan said.

'No,' Mitch said, 'ah, anyway, I had her all signed up. It was fourteen nights. You know what that cost me? Three thousand dollars.'

'Now,' Cogan said, 'that really oughta do it. I wouldn't pay no broad three thousand to do anything. I wouldn't care what she could do. I wouldn't pay it.'

'I didn't care,' Mitch said. 'I was still with the union then, and the guys that had the jobs, they were always very nice to me. You didn't have no wildcats or anything, well, see what I mean? I didn't care. So it's a lot. I'm not in *love* with the girl, right? I only give her for when I'm there.'

'She's still a great-looking girl, though,' Cogan said.

'She is,' Mitch said. 'That fuckin' Sammy. The night you saw her, what'd she have on?'

'Tell you the truth,' Cogan said, 'I didn't notice what she was wearing, so much's what she was wearing it on. Some yellow thing or something. You could see quite a lot.'

'There's quite a lot to see,' Mitch said. 'The night Sammy comes by, right? She's got this gray thing on. It's like silk, and it's gray, and there isn't any back on it and she's got these mammoth tits, she's really something. I could've beat up five guys with the horn I had on, and I, I had her all them other nights, right? So Sammy comes up and I introduce them, and how long am I there for and how long's he there for, and I'm not really paying attention or anything, we're having some wine and so I asked him to sit down. And pretty soon I got to go to the Men's. So I go, and I'm gone a pretty long time, because I got this huge prong on and I gotta practically stand on my head if I wanna piss in the hopper and not in my own fuckin' mouth, and still, I wanna be careful with it, you know? It was really big. I don't think I could've blinked. I don't think I had no skin left. She's good, Sunny's good about that. Sunny can't get you up, you're probably dead. But this's the last time, and she's not gonna have to. Because I'm all ready to go, I can ever get through dinner. My friend, I don't care what you say, I seen every kind of ass there is, you know that?'

'You've seen it this week,' Cogan said. 'You been here, what, three days, what I hear you had a look at most of the ass there is in Boston.'

'I like it,' Mitch said. 'That's what it is, I like it. It's like, it's a hobby with me, you know? I never do nothing when I'm home. Nothing But that's why, I go the races. Once a year, I go to the races, and I get laid. Only this year, probably I'm not goin' the races.'

'I couldn't do it,' Cogan said. 'I'd get all fucked out. You, I think you're probably in good shape. I wouldn't, I couldn't fuck for three days, is all. I couldn't do it.'

'I was your age,' Mitch said, 'I felt exactly the same way.'

'Sure,' Cogan said. 'I got work I got to do.'

Mitch drank from the glass. 'I used to think the same way,' he said. 'Then, I dunno *when* it happened, I dunno *why* it happened. I just started doing it. I went down there, the very first time I went down there, I got the suite. I was having a terrible time with Margie, and she finds out about it and she's giving me all kinds of hell about it, you asked her and she'd tell you she drinks because I go down there. Well, it was her or me. But I can tell you, boy, you want ass, get yourself a, there's no ass inna whole wide world like a young Jewish girl that's hookin'.'

'I'll keep it in mind,' Cogan said.

'That broad,' Mitch said, 'she was in Oberlin, she was in college, right? And she quit. Whaddaya think of that?' He drank.

'You're gonna be all right,' Cogan said, 'tomorrow or the next night?'

'I'm all right, right now,' Mitch said. 'Christ sake. Lemme alone, willya? Well, she quit. And she took up hookin'. Now you get a broad like that, they really go right to work on it, you know? And they get so, they really know their fuckin' business. That broad, Sunny, she's not, she isn't half my wife's age and she knew things which, if Margie knew them she'd go down the station and turn herself in. She really would.

'So, I come back the table,' Mitch said. 'I finally get rid of that wine without pissing on my own fuckin' chin and they're both there and Sammy's being very polite and all, and finally he leaves and then we finish and I thought to fuckin' God, I can pole-vault up to the room with just what I got of my own, and we go up there and I want to tell you, three thousand bucks, it's not cheap and I don't care whether you got it or not, it's fuckin' expensive, but it's worth it, it was honestly worth it. I give her three for the whole time and that night alone, it was worth it all. Only, I don't tell *her* that, of course.'

'Mitch,' Cogan said.

'So the next day I get up,' Mitch said. 'I also get up, but I hadda twelve-thirty plane so it's just a quickie. Just a quickie with Sunny's about nine times better'n a whole fuckin' date with another broad. And then I go down and I get some steam, and I come back up and I got to give her the rest of the money. See, you give them half when you get there and then when you're through, down there, you give them the rest. So I say, I tell her, I really appreciate it, I know what this means, all that time right out in one chunk and all. And she tells me, see, she's out of circulation and everything, she tells me: "It's all right," there isn't any problem, and I give her the money and everything, and she's leaving, and, well, she's gonna stay with Sammy the next two weeks and he's hitting her four for it. That cocksucker.'

'Look,' Cogan said, 'this after, I'm supposed to meet a kid, all right? I think I got a guy that can take you around and all.'

'I can't go out,' Mitch said.

'I didn't mean fuckin' around,' Cogan said. 'You come up here to do something. For that. I was gonna talk to him and then if I'm satisfied, he can do something without having his brother hold his hand all the time, I was gonna bring him up here and talk about it with you.'

'It's all right with me,' Mitch said.

'Well,' Cogan said, 'I'm glad to hear that. Only, it's not all right with me. Because you're not gonna be able, be able to make it tonight, and I don't want this kid thinking about things too long, he's liable to go tell his brother.'

'Aw right,' Mitch said, 'where the fuck is he? Get him up here and we'll set the guy up.'

'You,' Cogan said, 'I'll tell you what you're gonna do, right? You're goin' to bed.'

'I'm not tired,' Mitch said.

'You sure as hell look tired to me,' Cogan said. 'You go to fuckin' bed. And, it's two-thirty now, you shit. I'm gonna call you at seven-thirty and I better wake you up, because if I don't, I'm gonna drop a dime on a couple cops I know and they'll take you back where you're supposed to be.'

'Yeah,' Mitch said.

'No ass,' Cogan said, 'no more booze, no nothing. You get your-self a shower and go to bed and I'll wake you up and tell you where you gotta be, right?'

'I don't take orders from shits like you,' Mitch said.

16

The driver turned off the ignition of the silver Toronado and waited for Cogan to cross the trolley tracks behind Cronin's in Cambridge. When Cogan got in, the driver said: 'You know, I hate to be a burden to anybody, but life'd be a whole lot easier for me if you could bring yourself to use a telephone now and then to talk about things. They've got pay phones now, anybody can use them. I bet I can even give you two or three numbers in Providence alone that're pay phones, and if you wanted to call me up and talk to me about something, all you'd have to do is call me up and say which one. This running back and forth every time somebody gets a runny nose's raising hell with me. My wife's sick and one of the kids's sick and my practice's going to hell, and that isn't even enough for you, one of the last good Saturdays we're likely to see in a long time I think, and I had to give up nine holes to come up here and talk to you. That's all I seem to do, lately, cancel appointments and drive up here to talk to you.'

'You oughta talk to the man, Albert,' Cogan said. 'Sounds to me like you're the kind of man, deserves a raise. Tell him to get in touch with me. I'll put in a good word for you.'

'You're all heart,' the driver said. 'Okay, I'm here. Let's have the latest bad news. What's messed up now?'

'Well,' Cogan said, 'we seem to have a little problem.'

'We're not supposed to have any more little problems,' the driver said, 'no little problems at all. I've talked to him and we've done everything you asked. No problems at all, big or little. Tell me one thing you asked for, that we didn't go along with.'

'Nothing,' Cogan said. 'Only, there's a couple things I didn't know.'

'Tell me about it,' the driver said.

'Mitch,' Cogan said. 'He can't do it. I had things pretty well lined up for tonight. I know where Amato's gonna be, and I'm pretty sure I can find out before dark where the kid that I'm sure of's going to be. But at least we had Amato lined up. We could do a double, if things went right, or we'd at least get the Squirrel and he's the big one anyway. But Mitch can't do it.'

'You asked for him,' the driver said. 'You and Dillon both asked for him. You said you couldn't do it, and Dillon of course can't. We got you what you asked for.'

'What I asked for,' Cogan said, 'was, I didn't know this, see? I wanted Mitch the way he was a year, a couple years ago. He's fuckin' worthless now.'

'What's the matter with him?' the driver said.

'The first thing I heard about,' Cogan said, 'he's got this beef down in Maryland. He thinks he's gonna do a bit for it and he's

187

scared of the bit because he thinks his wife's gonna dump him if he does. Which, from what he tells me, she is, and even if she wasn't, he hasn't got any idea he's gonna really enjoy doing the bit anyway.'

'I don't see what that's got to do with this,' the driver said.

'It don't seem to, at first,' Cogan said, 'except that he's not supposed to go any place but Maryland without getting permission, and naturally he didn't, come up here, so he's afraid to go out and he stays inna room all the time. Because they'll heave him in just for being here.

'Anyway,' Cogan said, 'he's staying inside and he's fucking everything that jumps.'

'He said,' the driver said, 'when I told him you wanted Mitch, he said it was all right, but it might be the best idea if you could find some way to keep the fellow locked in the bathroom all the time he's here. Well, what is it? Won't he come out?'

'He'll come out if we want him to,' Cogan said. 'I don't think we do. When he landed here he wanted me to get him a broad, and I thought, what the fuck business is it of mine? I thought he wanted a broad. I called up a guy, guy got him a broad. Beautiful. But what he did was get that broad to give him the names of some other broads, and these aren't hookers in from Lawrence for the night, either. These're girls that see a lot of guys and talk to a lot of guys, and they all know he's in town by now, and that isn't gonna help us. This kid I sent around, I asked for one that's just getting started and doesn't know anybody from a pisshole in the snow. But he also found Polly, he tells me, and there isn't one guy in town doesn't know Polly, and this silly bastard hadda fight with her, for Christ sake. That girl talks to cops.'

'Has he lost his mind?' the driver said.

'I think,' Cogan said, 'I think there's a limited amount of shit a guy can take, and Mitch went over his limit. When I met him he was drinking up a storm, and I said something to him and he told me, it scares the shit out of him when he's got to fly and he can't sleep the night before and he's got to get something in him so he can sleep. So, okay, and I could see there's a lot of things bothering him. Let the guy do what he wants.

'Well,' Cogan said, 'that was three days ago, and what he didn't fuck in them three days, he drank. When I left him, he was drunk. Two-thirty in the afternoon, and he was finishing up a fight with another heavy cruiser he got from some place. Really drunk, talking and everything, he can't remember what year things happened, for Christ sake, and I chew him out for it and he's gonna go right out in his skivvies and do the job now. He won't shut up.'

'Have you talked to Dillon?' the driver said. 'Is Dillon well enough to talk to?'

'Told me he went out for a walk yesterday,' Cogan said. 'Said he's feeling much stronger, he had a good dinner last night and watched TV. Yeah. Dillon thinks what I think. This guy'll blow the whole thing if we don't do something. He'll get another broad and another jug up there, and if one of the ones he had already didn't get the word onna street, the next one will. We need that guy out of town yesterday, is what we need.'

'Well,' the driver said, 'you invited him up here. Send him back.'

'He wouldn't go,' Cogan said. 'He's hungry for the dough, said he really needs dough. Lost his job or something and everything. He wouldn't go if I told him. I don't think he'd do anything I told him, unless he was so drunk he couldn't think of anything else to do. Which he probably is.'

'I can't get in touch with him today,' the driver said.

189

'It's nothing like that,' Cogan said. 'What I got in mind, I'm gonna get him grabbed.'

'Turn him in,' the driver said. 'Won't he talk?'

'If he thought it was me that did it, he might,' Cogan said. 'What I was thinking of, this guy I know, he's got this one broad that is tops at setting guys up. She gets in real fights with them, and they give her their fuckin' teeth to get her out of the room before the cops come. I was thinking of sending her up there, see, I told him, no more ass, he's going to work, but he's so drunk he won't remember whether he had somebody send her up or not, and he'd take her if he didn't. Now, this hotel, they don't exactly keep tabs on people, but it's a good place and they're not gonna want no whore fights going on in there, and he'll get busted for that and pretty soon they'll revoke bail on him and back he'll go.'

'Kind of rough on him,' the driver said.

'Not actually,' Cogan said. 'Actually, I think it's the best thing for him. He's gonna kill himself if he does this much longer. He won't get enough potato jack in the can to kill him, and if he's not in the can he'll kill us.'

'I suppose he really should talk to Mitch's people,' the driver said.

'Albert,' Cogan said, 'how're they gonna know?'

'Ah,' Albert said. 'I can tell him, I suppose.'

'If you want,' Cogan said. 'Let him make up his own mind.'

'Okay,' the driver said, 'do it. Now, that leaves us with Amato.'

'I come up with something, I think,' Cogan said. 'I think I can set him up myself.'

'I thought you couldn't,' the driver said. 'I thought he knew you.'

'He does,' Cogan said. 'He also knows the kid, one of the kids he used on the job. And that kid, I bet, is gonna know where Amato's gonna be, the next few nights or so.'

'Will he do it?' the driver said.

'I was waiting for you,' Cogan said, 'I started thinking. Yeah, I think I know a way.'

'Will he be all right?' the driver said.

'Oh,' Cogan said, 'you can't tell.'

'Well, it's serious, isn't it?' the driver said. 'It's a serious question.'

Cogan stared at the driver. 'For a while,' he said. 'Not long, but a while. Talk to the man.'

17

Frankie sat at the first bar downstairs in the Carnaby Street, late in the afternoon. He leaned back on the bentwood stool and watched the waitresses chatting, idle until customers came.

Cogan hung the pilled suede coat on a peg and sat down next to Frankie. He ordered a beer.

'Heineken?' the bartender said.

'Yeah,' Cogan said.

'Bottle or draft?' the bartender said.

'I don't give a shit,' Cogan said. 'Draft.'

'They always do that,' Frankie said.

'It's a pain in the ass,' Cogan said. 'I wouldn't've come in here, I thought I was gonna have to go through something like that.'

The bartender put a frosted mug in front of Cogan.

'I would,' Frankie said. 'This guy, I dunno how he does it, he's got to have the best-built girls in Boston working for him. I come in here every day.'

'I know,' Cogan said.

Frankie looked at him. 'I never seen you before in here,' he said. 'I don't know you.'

'Didn't say you did,' Cogan said. 'Very few guys know me. I'm just a guy, is all. I never been in here before in my life.'

'How'd you happen to come in today?' Frankie said.

'Looking for you,' Cogan said. 'I was looking for you and a guy told me, he said you told him you come in here a lot, 'round this time of day, see if you can get up nerve enough, talk to a girl. So I came in. Simple, huh?'

'Who's the guy?' Frankie said.

'Just a guy,' Cogan said, 'guy, a friend of yours, actually. Knows a little about you, told me where to look you up. Well, he didn't tell me himself. He told a guy, and the guy was up here and he told me. Because I asked the guy, this friend of yours.'

'Who's this friend?' Frankie said.

'China,' Cogan said.

'Never heard of nobody by that name,' Frankie said. He finished his beer and started to straighten up.

Cogan put his right hand on Frankie's right arm. 'China'll be surprised to hear that,' he said, 'very surprised. Here's a guy, concerned about you, your friends're concerned about you, you know that, Frankie? They're worried. Guys like China. China was really, he, well, he insisted I hadda go and talk to you, is what he did. I wasn't sure I oughta bother you, you know? Got yourself a place and everything? "Sounds like he's doing all right to me," is what I said. "No reason I should go around and bother him." You have got a place, haven't you, Frankie?'

'Yeah,' Frankie said.

'Somewhere south of New Hampshire, I bet,' Cogan said.

'Right onna peg,' Frankie said.

'Norwood, to be exact,' Cogan said. 'Why'd you do that, alla them trucks?'

'I dunno,' Frankie said.

'Now whyn't you relax a little, Frankie, okay?' Cogan said. 'You know how it is when a guy, when China wants a guy to do something, you got to do it, is all, China's all down there, locked up and everything, he's gotta depend on his friends, do the right things for guys he's worried about. I'd be embarrassed in front of China, I hadda tell him, he ever found out, a guy he wanted me to talk to, I didn't talk to him. You know how China is.'

Frankie leaned back again.

'Have another beer,' Cogan said. 'Look at the girls. Jesus, I dunno how you can stand the noise out there. Still, I suppose, guys got all kinds of reasons for doing things. Gotta car, too, I understand.'

'Yeah,' Frankie said.

'Lemme give you some advice, all right?' Cogan said.

Frankie did not answer.

'I had one of them things myself,' Cogan said, 'they first come out. You got the hood scoops, right?' Frankie did not answer.

'Ah, come on,' Cogan said, 'you got the green Geetoh with the scoops. Don't fuck around with me, right?'

Frankie nodded.

'You're gonna have trouble with it,' Cogan said, 'couple months or so. January, when it gets cold. Fuckin' thing won't run. It'll start but it won't run. You can do anything you want to it, it won't run, and when it's really cold, down around seven, eight below, it won't start.

'Now lemme tell you what you got to do,' Cogan said. 'You got to pack them scoops. Mine just had the one, the split one in the middle. But, well, you got the two, I bet you're still gonna have the same trouble, the car just won't warm up. You're gonna have to pack them scoops. It's the scoops. Your engine can't get warm in that thing when it's cold unless you run it about ninety miles an hour the minute you get her going, and you do that, you're gonna bend a fuckin' valve, is all. What I used to do, I used to put masking tape right over them scoops. Looks like hell, but it works. Got that? Masking tape.'

Frankie nodded.

'You see what I mean,' Cogan said.

'Uh,' Frankie said, 'uh, no. No, I don't.'

'Your friends,' Cogan said. 'Your friends're worried about you. See? I even heard, you're carrying.'

'Fuck, no,' Frankie said.

'Well,' Cogan said, 'now, that's good. Because, you wanna be careful about that. You, what, you been out a month?'

'Six weeks,' Frankie said.

'Right,' Cogan said. 'Onna robbery thing, am I right?'

'Yeah,' Frankie said.

'Well, there you are,' Cogan said, 'and that's why it's such a good thing, you're not carrying. You know how those guys are. They're gonna be measuring your dick every time somebody pulls a job looks anything like what you did. You think they don't know you're out?'

'Nope,' Frankie said.

'And of course,' Cogan said, 'they're not gonna get nothing on you, because you're not doing nothing, am I right?'

'Just havin' a beer and watchin' the girls,' Frankie said.

'Sure,' Cogan said. 'Nothing wrong with that. But, they pick you up, even though you didn't pull a job, you're carrying, they're gonna run you again.'

'I know that,' Frankie said.

'Well,' Cogan said, 'that's good. That shows, your friends that're worried about you, shows them you must've grown up some since you went in.'

Frankie looked at Cogan. 'Grown up some?' he said. 'A dog'd get born and live and die in the time I was in.'

'Well,' Cogan said, 'yeah, you're right. But, maybe even since you got out. Maybe you grown up some since then.'

'Well,' Frankie said, 'I finally got laid.'

'That's good,' Cogan said. 'How was it?'

'Not so good,' Frankie said. 'Matter of fact, it was kind of shitty. I naturally got some broad that's been fuckin' since they found out how to do it, and I naturally shot my mouth off all over the place and I got through and she told me I'm a lousy lay. I'm gonna keep at it, though. I figure, can't be too tough to get the hang of it, and there must be some reason, there's so many people running around doing it.'

'That's the idea,' Cogan said. He made a sucking noise with his tongue and his teeth. 'Jesus,' he said, 'that's too bad. If I'd've only run into you sooner. I should've got on this right away, when I first get the word from China and them. I knew a guy could've helped you along that line. Really knew some great broads. But he's dead.'

'Oh yeah?' Frankie said.

'Yeah,' Cogan said. 'It's too bad. You maybe saw it inna paper.

Somebody whacked him out the other night. Markie Trattman. Nice guy. A real nice guy, and what that guy didn't know about getting broads, nobody knew.'

'Must've fucked the wrong one, I guess,' Frankie said.

'Yeah,' Cogan said, 'it was either that or something else. He got somebody pissed off, that's for sure. That's the way it is with most of them guys, I think, that get whacked. They get somebody pissed and then something happens. You got to be careful, these days. You do something, looks perfectly all right to you, and the right guy gets pissed off for no reason at all and you're in the shit. Look at China. How long you known China?'

'China?' Frankie said. 'Ten years or so, I guess.'

'Well,' Cogan said, 'that's long enough. Now there's a guy, you should've heard what they're saying about China, year or so ago.'

'I did,' Frankie said.

'Yeah,' Cogan said, 'and, knowing China, you got to know, it's not true. China'd eat shit before he'd talk to anybody. But the trouble is, some asshole gets it in his head that something's going on or something, and he starts spreading stuff around about China, and of course nobody asks any questions or does anything smart like that. They just talk and talk and talk and pretty soon China's getting all this static, and he wasn't even doing anything.

'Now,' Cogan said, 'China's a smart bastard. He's down there and he knows he's gotta see somebody and see them quick. So he gets himself a habe or something and they bring him up here and he gets a chance to get the word to a few guys and somebody got in to see him and he told him: "Look, I'm gonna get a shiv up my ass if somebody doesn't start stopping all this talk and shit, you know? And, I'm not gonna stand still for that. If I gotta protect myself, I'm gonna have to go to somebody and start telling them things, and I don't want to do that, all right?" So the guy comes out and he puts it around and China's all right again with everybody. See, that's what I mean. China's a smart bastard, knows how to protect his ass. Markie, well, he knew a lot about broads, but I guess he didn't know nothing about protecting his ass.'

'Kind of hard to cover your ass,' Frankie said, 'you don't even know some guy's after you for dipping your wick. Kind of hard.'

'Yeah,' Cogan said, 'but there's other things it could've been, it could've happened. Now Markie, Markie ran a game. And it got knocked over. You know that?'

'I think I heard something about it,' Frankie said.

'Yeah,' Cogan said. He drank his beer. To the bartender he said: 'Lemme have another one.' To Frankie he said: 'Want another one?'

'I think I'm set,' Frankie said.

'Right,' Cogan said. He accepted the fresh mug and drank from it. 'Good,' he said, wiping his mouth. 'Nothin' like a cold beer, I always say. Well, now, Trattman always ran that game, right? He had a game running ever since anybody can remember. And he had a game, went over before. He got robbed before. And you know something?' Cogan said. 'It was actually Markie, had it knocked over.'

'Maybe he did it again,' Frankie said.

'There's a lot of silly shits that're running around, saying that,' Cogan said. 'I actually heard some of that talk myself. And it pissed me off. Because, Markie wasn't no particular friend of mine, you understand, I bet I didn't talk to him more'n once, twice, in my whole life. So, he gets himself in some kind of trouble, it's not up to me, go around and straighten him out. Who am I? Just a guy he knows. Why's he gonna listen to me? But since then, I thought,

I should've. I really should've. Because there wasn't nothing to that talk and shit. Markie wouldn't do that again. He was way too smart for that. But see, that's what I mean. He hadda *know*, he hadda know the kind of talk that was going around, and he should've been smart enough, he heard some of it, like China, you know? Do something about it. So some silly shit don't decide he's gonna make himself all kinds of friends, all he's gotta do is whack Trattman out. It's a crazy fuckin' world.

'See, Frankie,' Cogan said, turning slightly toward him, 'I think that's what China and them think, your friends, that're worried about you. They think, well, they dunno how much you grown up, since you got out, even. They think you need somebody around, knows about things, advise you.'

'Yeah,' Frankie said.

'Teach you how to cover your ass,' Cogan said. 'See, like I was saying, it's not what you been doing so much's it is what guys think you been doing, and that's what you got to look out for, and when it happens, well, you got to be prepared to do something.'

'Yeah,' Frankie said.

'So,' Cogan said in a lower voice, 'where's he gonna be, tomorrow night?'

'Who?' Frankie said.

'Johnny Amato,' Cogan said. 'Tomorrow night. Where's he gonna be?'

'I dunno,' Frankie said.

'Frank,' Cogan said, 'you got to keep in mind what I told you. Your friends're worried about you. You wanna finally get laid right, it's your friends, they wanna see you get the chance, you know what I mean? And it's your friends, wanna know where Squirrel's gonna be.'

'This's the first time I seen you,' Frankie said.

'New friends're best,' Cogan said. 'Your other one, there, you can't depend on him, you know? Look at what he got you in before. All that time. You could've been out getting a decent piece of ass, 'stead of pounding sand up yours and everything.'

'I don't know who the fuck you are,' Frankie said.

'Very few guys do,' Cogan said. 'Oh, China, maybe, and, oh yeah: Dillon. Dillon knows me. You're, you strike me as a pretty intelligent guy. Want me to call Dillon for you, and you can talk to him, see who I am? There's not much to find out, I can tell you that. But you can talk to him. Wanna talk to Dillon?'

'No,' Frankie said.

'Well okay,' Cogan said. 'Where's he gonna be? I know you're gonna know, if you don't know now.'

'I haven't got no idea,' Frankie said. 'I seen John three or four times since I got out. I don't know what he does, nights. Goes home, I guess.'

'Okay,' Cogan said. He finished his beer. 'See you around, Frankie, my friend.' He started to get off the stool.

'Wait a minute,' Frankie said.

'There's things,' Cogan said, 'there's things that won't wait. You tell me, you don't know. Okay, I accept that. But I got something to do. I got to find a guy that knows.'

'Where John's gonna be tomorrow night,' Frankie said.

'And something else now, I guess,' Cogan said. 'Like where you're gonna be, the day after. You gonna be here again? Gonna come in about three-thirty, drink about four beers, hang around until you eat, leave and go up Pagliacci's like you always do, see what's still breathing enough to fuck, go home around midnight, one o'clock? That what you're gonna be doing day after tomorrow?

Or are you gonna be doing something else, so it takes me a couple, three days extra? It's not gonna matter. You could just save me a lot of time, is all.'

Frankie said nothing

Cogan got off the stool. He rested his forearms on the back of it. 'Look,' he said, 'you gotta be realistic, right, kid? You gotta be. I know the guy. I also know what's goin' through your head. He's, you think he's a friend of yours, right? You probably, you probably got something lined up with him right now, am I right?'

Frankie did not answer.

'It don't matter,' Cogan said. 'I know how you feel. But you think, I bet you figured, that Trattman thing, it was gonna work, right?'

Frankie did not answer.

'Them things,' Cogan said, 'lemme tell you something, kid: them things, they never work. Guys with bright ideas, you know? Like Squirrel. They all know the end-around, and they're not gonna get something and work it steady and make it work and make it pay. Not them. He's always been like this, always been looking for a hustle, and guys like him, all they ever do is fuck things up. For everybody else.'

'Trattman got hit,' Frankie said.

'There's all kinds of reasons for things,' Cogan said. 'Guys get whacked for doing things, guys get whacked for not doing things, it don't matter. The only thing matters is if you're the guy that's gonna get whacked. That's the only fuckin' thing.'

Frankie nodded.

'You,' Cogan said, 'you're one of the few guys that know, right?'

'I dunno,' Frankie said.

'Yes you do,' Cogan said. 'You know very fuckin' well. You, you got a choice. You're gonna be one of the guys that gets whacked out or else you're not. You know that. It's just a matter of time, now, my friend. Just a matter of time. Him first and then you. That's the way you're going.'

Frankie did not answer.

'Except you're in a position,' Cogan said, 'you're in a position very few of them guys ever get in. You can do something about it. I known very few guys inna position like that.'

Frankie did not answer.

'Frank,' Cogan said, 'I hope you don't think, I'm shittin' you.'

'Look,' Frankie said, 'who the fuck are you? I never saw you before in my life, all of a sudden you're telling me all these things. What the fuck do I know? Maybe you're not even here. I don't know nothing.'

'Kid,' Cogan said, 'I hate to see you go like this. China says you're all right. And you're going for fuckin' nothin'.'

'I'm ...' Frankie said, 'Jesus, I dunno.'

'Lemme ask you something,' Cogan said, 'and you think about this, all right? You think, I was to go down Wollaston and see him, there, right now, I was to leave here and drive down there and see him and say: "Squirrel, it's you or Frankie. Who's it gonna be?" You think he'd even think about it? You think he would?'

'I dunno,' Frankie said.

'You asshole,' Cogan said. 'An asshole like you, it's no wonder you did time. You *fuck kin asshole*. You haven't got no brains at all.'

'Look,' Frankie said, 'look, I ...'

'I haven't got to look,' Cogan said. 'Look, I know what's going on. I know what I got to do. I need a right guy.'

Frankie's mouth worked. He did not say anything.

'If I get a right guy,' Cogan said, 'I told them this, by the way,

I said: 'There's two ways this thing can go. The hard way is, I do them both. The other way, I only gotta do one guy.' I took a lot of shit for that. You know how I got them to go along with this? China. China says you're all right. So, I always like China, I can do something for China, I'm gonna. China don't want. you hit. Very loud on that point. Says you're a good guy, kind of guy it's good to have around. Okay. But you know where China is. All he can do is come up here and talk. He can't actually do nothing for a guy.'

'No,' Frankie said.

'I can do something for a guy,' Cogan said. 'I don't have to, but I can. Now make the pick, kid, and make it right now. I'm gonna do China a favor, I'm not gonna do China a favor. Don't matter to me.'

'Lemme think,' Frankie said.

'Nope,' Cogan said, 'no thinking. Go or no go, right now. I got to get going.'

Frankie exhaled heavily. 'I don't know,' he said. 'I don't know if I can do this.'

'Can you do the other thing?' Cogan said.

Frankie hesitated. 'No,' he said.

'Well,' Cogan said, 'that's the selection. So, I guess you know, then.'

'What've I gotta do?' Frankie said.

'You gotta find out where he's gonna be,' Cogan said.

'I already know that,' Frankie said. 'We're, he asked me what I was gonna be doing, he's gonna be some place and he wants to call me or something. I know where he's gonna be. He's got a girl. He told me that, before. I told him I was gonna be home, I'd be home.'

'You're not gonna be,' Cogan said.

'I'm not?' Frankie said.

'No,' Cogan said.

'Where …' Frankie said.

'You're gonna be with me,' Cogan said, 'and we're gonna be where he's gonna be.'

'Jesus,' Frankie said, 'I can't do that. He sees me, it's all over. He'll know, something's wrong. I can't do that. I'll tell you, I'll tell you where he's gonna be. I'll do that. But, he's a friend of mine. I can't do that.'

'Okay,' Cogan said, 'okay. That's, you made the other choice then, I guess.'

Frankie stared at Cogan. Cogan did not move. Frankie said: 'Have I really got to do that?'

Cogan nodded.

'All of it?' Frankie said.

Cogan nodded.

'I got to be there and everything?'

Cogan nodded.

'It's not,' Frankie said, 'it's not like, there was anything I could do, anybody else inna world couldn't do. It's not that. You, there must be hundreds of guys, you can get. You don't need me.'

'Wrong,' Cogan said. He put his hand on Frankie's shoulder. 'Frank,' he said, 'it's not like I don't understand what's on your mind, right? But this thing's a problem. And part of it, it's partly your fault. You made a mistake. Now you gotta, you got to do the right thing. You gotta show, you understand, you made a mistake, and you gotta make things right. Otherwise, guys know you made a mistake, right? And that's when they're gonna want somebody to do something, like with Trattman. He never did the right thing.'

Frankie nodded.

18

Frankie drove the Gold Duster quickly through the arch with the orange lanterns into the curving drives of Stuart Manor. The apartment complexes were two- story, the first of vertical redwood planks, the second stucco, half-timbered. The parking areas were filled with Volkswagens, Camaros, Mustangs and Barracudas. There were coach lights with orange bulbs above each door.

'Jee-zuss,' Cogan said, 'I finally made it. I'm in ghinny heaven.'

The small tires on the Duster howled as Frankie took it through the curves to the back of the third complex. 'It's a singles place,' he said. 'You're supposed to live here if you wanna get laid.'

'I'd have to get awful horny to drive to New Hampshire to get laid,' Cogan said.

'It's not that far,' Frankie said. 'I thought the same thing, but Johnny got tied up one night and I hadda bring her back up here. It's not that far.'

'Seems far to me,' Cogan said. 'This, this just proves it to me. The guy's a shit.'

'He don't have no control, where the girls live,' Frankie said. He pulled into an empty space and shut off the engine and the lights.

'He don't have no control,' Cogan said. 'Period.'

'Jackie,' Frankie said, 'he's really not a bad guy, you know? He's not a bad guy at all.'

Cogan slouched down in the seat. The suede coat piled up around him at the neck. He shut his eyes. 'None of 'em are,' he said. 'They're all nice guys. They just get to thinking, you know?'

'He was always all right to me,' Frankie said.

'Sure,' Cogan said. 'Got you almost six years inna fuckin' slammer.'

'That wasn't his fault,' Frankie said.

'Kid,' Cogan said, 'when somebody does something, and some-body, he gets somebody else, and they go to fuckin' jail for it, it's his fault. That's the rule.'

'It wasn't his fault,' Frankie said.

'Then this isn't your fault,' Cogan said. 'If that wasn't his fault, this isn't your fault.'

'He didn't mean it,' Frankie said.

'Hasn't got nothing to do with it,' Cogan said, 'nothing at all.'

A blue Rallye Nova passed behind the Duster.

'That them?' Cogan said.

'Nah,' Frankie said. 'John, John's got a Riviera.'

'I know what he's got,' Cogan said. 'What I want to know is, that them?'

'Nope,' Frankie said. 'I'd've said if it was. You got him wrong, you know. That jail thing, he had it worse'n I did, his family and all.'

'He's not gonna have to do it again,' Cogan said.

'He stood up,' Frankie said. 'He could've blamed it all on us.'

'In a way,' Cogan said, 'he did.'

'He did not,' Frankie said. 'He never said shit.'

'He didn't say shit about you, maybe,' Cogan said. 'He still called somebody up.'

'About what?' Frankie said. 'What'd he call up?'

'He knows how you do things,' Cogan said. 'He knows how you're supposed to, anyway. He knows.'

'What's he know?' Frankie said.

'Ever hear of the Doctor?' Cogan said.

'Yeah, yeah,' Frankie said. 'Dillon says he's dead. I know.'

'When're you talking to Dillon?' Cogan said.

'I didn't talk to him,' Frankie said. 'Johnny told me that, said Dillon said the Doctor's dead.'

'He is dead,' Cogan said.

'Okay,' Frankie said, 'you and Johnny and Dillon, the whole bunch of you say the Doctor's dead. Big deal.'

'The Squirrel says he's dead,' Cogan said.

'Johnny said Dillon told him, the Doctor's dead,' Frankie said.

'That shit,' Cogan said. 'That fuckin' shit.'

A brown Maverick Grabber passed behind the Duster.

'Still not them,' Frankie said. 'Why?'

'Because he knows it himself,' Cogan said. 'He knows very fuckin' well, the Doctor's dead.'

'How's he know?' Frankie said.

'He paid a man,' Cogan said, 'he paid a man, five thousand dollars, get the Doctor dead.'

'Bull*shit*,' Frankie said.

'What's his wife's name,' Cogan said, 'you want me to tell you, tell you what she looks like and everything, used to wear them big gold-hoop earrings? Connie.'

'So what?' Frankie said.

'That's the broad that delivered the money,' Cogan said. 'For the Doctor's ass. Think he'd pay that if he didn't know it was done?'

Frankie did not answer.

'You know why, Frank, he got the Doctor?' Cogan said.

'Yeah,' Frankie said, 'I know.'

'Sure,' Cogan said. 'Doctor made a mistake, did something he wasn't supposed to. That's why.'

'Well,' Frankie said, 'he did.'

'Sure he did,' Cogan said. 'So'd he.'

'It's not the same thing,' Frankie said. 'It's not the same thing at all.'

A maroon Monte Carlo passed behind the Duster.

'Sure it is,' Cogan said, 'the Doctor got taken out for getting everybody in the shit. And that's what him and you did. You just thought, the only thing that was different, you thought Trattman'd get blamed for it.'

A red Capri passed behind the Duster.

'That's what I mean,' Cogan said. 'You don't get away with things like that. Trattman was the same way. Thought he was gonna get away with it.'

'He did,' Frankie said. 'Once.'

'That's what I mean,' Cogan said. 'You don't get away with nothing once, it happens again.'

The bronze Riviera passed behind the Duster.

'That's him,' Cogan said.

'I'm not sure,' Frankie said.

'Yes you are,' Cogan said. 'If you're not you got the first all-over hard-on in the world.' He opened his eyes and watched the Riviera. It pulled in beyond the back door of the complex.

'How long's he gonna be, kid?' Cogan said.

'I dunno,' Frankie said.

'Okay,' Cogan said, 'I asked you nice. Now, does he fuck her here or does he fuck her some place else?'

'She's got a roommate,' Frankie said. 'He knows a guy's got a motel in Haverhill.'

'Okay,' Cogan said, 'he's just gonna be friendly, then.' He watched as the door of the Riviera opened. He watched the long white leg of the girl. He watched Amato emerge from the building shadow and walk around the rear of the car. He watched Amato assist the girl from the car and shut the door.

Cogan reached down on the floor of the Duster with both hands and picked up a five-shot Winchester semiautomatic shotgun. He put it across his lap, steadying it with his right hand. With his left hand he took the key out of the Duster's ignition.

'Hey,' Frankie said, 'I mean, I was gonna start it and everything, we could get a start.'

'I know,' Cogan said, 'but, it's probably gonna get noisy around here, and I known guys, heard a lot of noise, they got too good a start and left somebody standing around with his thumb up his ass.'

Cogan watched Amato walk the girl to the door of the apartment complex.

Cogan opened the passenger door of the Duster, exposing the masking tape he had used to seal the interior light switch off, and slipped out of the car. Amato and the girl were thirty-five yards away, embracing at the door. Cogan crouched against the car, his

209

left elbow bracing against the top of the Duster's hood, the stock of the gun tight against his right shoulder.

Amato broke the embrace. The girl opened the door with a key. Amato waited on the step until the door closed behind her. She turned and waved at him, using only the fingers of her right hand. She was smiling. Amato waved back, in the same way. He turned away from the door. The girl vanished up the stairs.

Cogan fired the first deer slug at Amato. It caught him low on the abdomen and hurled him backward against the building. Cogan waited until Amato hit the top of his low arc. Then Cogan fired the second slug. It hit Amato higher, slightly above the belt on the left side, and went through him, taking an angle through his body which sent it through the glass panel of the door at his left. Cogan fired the third shot as Amato hit the wall of the building and started to sag down. It hit him in the middle of the chest, close to the base of his throat, and blew his chest apart. Amato toppled off to his own right in the low shrubbery.

Cogan backed up fast and got into the car. He shoved the shotgun into the back seat and stuck the key into the ignition. 'Now gimme that start,' he said.

The Duster leaped out of the space, taking the curves of the drive with the small tires screaming.

Three and one-half miles from Stuart Manor, Cogan said: 'You're going too fast.'

'Jesus,' Frankie said, 'they're gonna have all kinds of cops up here.' He held the Duster steady at seventy on the two-lane road.

'And one of them's gonna catch us,' Cogan said. 'Slow down.'

'I can't,' Frankie said.

'Kid,' Cogan said, 'look, slow down, all right?'

'I can't,' Frankie said. 'Honest to God, I can't.'

'Kid,' Cogan said, 'my car's in Massachusetts. We got a long way to go. I don't wanna get caught.'

'You wanna drive?' Frankie said.

'Yeah,' Cogan said.

Frankie pulled the Duster off on the shoulder of Route 64. He opened the driver's side door quickly and got out and trotted around the back of the car. Cogan slid across the seats. Frankie got in on the passenger side.

'Okay,' Cogan said, putting the Duster in drive, 'now, this means, you're gonna have to dump the gun.'

'Okay,' Frankie said.

Cogan stopped the Duster on the overpass at the Shawsheen River in Andover, Massachusetts. Frankie opened the passenger window and launched the gun out into the darkness. He started to close the window.

'Wait,' Cogan said.

There was a splash.

'Okay,' Cogan said. He put the Duster in gear again. 'Grass and stuff don't take care of prints,' he said. 'Water does.'

Cogan wheeled the Duster into the parking lot at the Northshore Plaza west of Salem. Behind Jordan Marsh's there was a blue LTD.

'You know what you got to do, now,' Cogan said, driving toward the LTD.

'Sure,' Frankie said. 'I go back down to where my car is and I leave this one and I go home.'

'You just leave it,' Cogan said.

'Oh Christ,' Frankie said, 'I wipe it down.'

'You're all right and everything,' Cogan said.

'*Yeah*,' Frankie said.

'Where's your car again?' Cogan said.

'For Christ sake,' Frankie said, 'it's down at, it's inna lot at Auburndale.'

'Just making sure,' Cogan said. 'You couldn't drive right, there. Some times guys forget.'

Cogan pulled the Duster up next to the LTD. The parking lot was lighted, but empty. Cogan opened the driver's side door. Frankie started sliding across the seat. Cogan got out. Frankie slid into the driver's seat. He put his hands on the wheel. Cogan held the door handle in his left hand. With his right hand he removed a Smith and Wesson thirty-eight Police Special, two-inch barrel, from beneath his coat.

'You're gonna remember, now,' Cogan said, holding the revolver below the level of the window.

'I know, I know,' Frankie said, 'I dump the fuckin' car and I get my car and I don't go too fast and I—'

Cogan raised the revolver and shot Frankie in the face, once. Frankie fell off toward the passenger seat. Cogan leaned in the window and put the muzzle of the revolver against Frankie's chest and fired four times, the powder blast burning Frankie's coat. The body shuddered with each shot.

Cogan put the revolver in the pocket of his car coat. He took unlined leather gloves from the other pocket, and a red handkerchief. He began to wipe the Duster down.

19

In the middle of the afternoon, Cogan parked his flame-painted white El Camino pickup beside the silver Toronado in the lot at the Holiday Inn at South Attleboro, Massachusetts. The sign next to the Toronado said: 'Welcome, South Jaycees.' Cogan went inside.

In the lounge the driver sat at the bar, dawdling with a large ginger ale. Cogan took the stool next to him.

'You're late,' the driver said.

'My mother used to tell me that,' Cogan said. ' "You'll be late for your own funeral." I hope so.'

'Had yourself quite a party,' the driver said.

'I do the best I can,' Cogan said. To the bartender he said: 'Beer.' The bartender filled a stein with Michelob.

'Everything's under control now, I take it,' the driver said. 'At long last.'

'You know,' Cogan said, 'for a guy I'm trying to help out and everything, you're awful hard to get along with. I could've made you drive up to Boston, you know. I hadda go to Framingham, I didn't have to come down here. I'm trying to be nice to you.'

'What the hell's wrong in Framingham,' the driver said, 'sky falling there or something?'

'Nah,' Cogan said. 'Stevie was outa hundred-millimeters and I had his car anyway and he had my truck, so I went out there and met him and give him some. I like to do a guy a favor now and then.'

'Do me a favor,' the driver said. 'Never do me any favors. I've seen how you work.'

'Tell you what,' Cogan said, 'gimme the money.'

The driver handed Cogan a thick white business envelope.

''Scuse me,' Cogan said. He slid off the stool.

'You going to *count* it?' the driver said.

'I gotta take a leak,' Cogan said. 'Just lemme alone, all right? You make me nervous. I get nervous, I always gotta take a leak. Have some more ginger ale, for Christ sake.'

Cogan went to the Men's Room. Cogan returned.

'You feel better?' the driver said.

'No,' Cogan said, 'there's only fifteen in there.'

'Three guys,' the driver said. 'I'm not sure, I had to ask him whether I should pay you for the kid or not. He said I should.'

'He was right, too,' Cogan said. 'That's five apiece.'

'Correct,' the driver said. 'That's what he told me to pay Mitch.'

'Yeah,' Cogan said, 'but the way I got it, Mitch got inna fight with a whore, the dumb shit, and now they got him in the can. Mitch couldn't do it. I come through for everybody on short notice. From now on, the price's ten.'

'Dillon only charges five,' the driver said. 'He told me that, too.'

'Not any more,' Cogan said.

'Look,' the driver said, 'you're filling in for Dillon. You get what Dillon gets. No more. Take it up with Dillon. I can't do anything about it.'

'You can't do anything about anything,' Cogan said. 'None of you guys can. Everything just goes haywire and everything, that's fine, you need somebody, get things straightened out. I'm just telling you, is all, it's gonna cost more, now on.'

'Tell Dillon,' the driver said. 'Take it up with him.'

'Dillon's dead,' Cogan said. 'Dillon died this morning.'

The driver was silent for a while. Then he said: 'He's going to be sorry to hear that.'

'No sorrier'n I am,' Cogan said.

The driver sipped his ginger ale. 'I assume,' he said, 'I assume. . . . What killed him?'

'I know the name of it,' Cogan said. 'I got home this morning, my wife left me a note, they took Dillon the hospital about midnight or so. They told me what it was. That's all I know.'

'He died in the hospital, then,' the driver said.

'Like I say,' Cogan said, 'I dunno what it is. All I know's what they told me. "Myocardial infarct." You know what that is? I guess it's the same thing, the heart trouble.'

'That's what he had,' the driver said. 'Well, how about that? Dillon's dead. Son of a bitch.'

'He wasn't a bad guy, actually,' Cogan said.

'No,' the driver said, 'no, I guess he wasn't. He wasn't a bad guy.'

'He always,' Cogan said, 'he never, well, I knew Dillon a long time, right? It was Dillon, really, got me started, said I oughta get something besides the booking, something that'd be around and like that, you know? He was the guy that really plugged me in. I knew Dillon a long time.'

'He knew him a long time too,' the driver said. 'He had a lot of respect for him.'

'Sure,' Cogan said, 'so'd I. You know why?'

'You were afraid of him?' the driver said.

'Nah,' Cogan said. He finished his beer. 'Nah, it wasn't that. It was, he knew the way things oughta be done, right?'

'So I'm told,' the driver said.

'And when they weren't,' Cogan said, 'he knew what to do.'

'And so do you,' the driver said.

'And so do I,' Cogan said.